novum **pro**

LUISA CARTEI

# I WILL MARRY
# Gary Barlow

novum ⬛ pro

www.novum-publishing.co.uk

© 2019 novum publishing

ISBN 978-3-99064-729-5
Editing: Ashleigh Brassfield, DipEdit
Cover photo:
Shelly Busby | https://unsplash.com/
Cover design, layout & typesetting:
novum publishing
Author's photo: Luisa Cartei

**www.novum-publishing.co.uk**

THIS IS A WORK OF FICTION,
LOOSELY BASED ON REAL EVENTS.

To my father, who taught me how to love.
To my cousin Sara, who told me "write!"
when we were only 7 years old.
To Gary, the man I wanted to marry.

*"When I was 5 years old, my mother always told me that happiness was the key to life. When I went to school, they asked me what I wanted to be when I grew up. I wrote down 'happy'. They told me I didn't understand the assignment, and I told them they didn't understand life."*

~ John Lennon ~

We've come so far and we've reached so high
And we've looked each day and night in the eye
And we're still so young and we hope for more
Never forget where you've come here from
Never pretend that it's all real
Someday soon this will all be someone else's dream
This will be someone else's dream

~ Take That, *Never Forget* ~

# PREFACE

## By Andrea Pinketts[1]

I have good news and bad news. Which one do you want first? OK, I'll choose for you. Let's hit the ground running with the bad news, so we can run it over and move on. I've been diagnosed with a poorly-differentiated squamous cell carcinoma. Poorly-differentiated? I took it as an insult, for a man like me, who stoutly defends difference as the pillar of any kind of union. Don't you worry, though; I intend to turn the cancer inside out, like a sock inside a sweaty, stinky Adidas. The good news is that the book I've just read is bright, even anti-cancer, in a way. Actually, the fact that the main character Alice's father is an empathic oncologist is comforting in itself.

Now that I've talked about my private life, let's move on and talk about what is public and published. Do you believe me? No? Good. After reading "I Will Marry Gary Barlow" by Luisa Cartei, whom I've never met but hope to soon, I'm pervaded by a sense of love and friendship.

Alice, the main character of the novel, crazily chases and manages to catch the ugliest guy of Take That (*Ciapà chi*[2], as we would say in Milanese dialect.) I know that such a distilled, sketched plot could seem like bullshit, but it isn't. It's the condensation of a decade, which has been skilfully summarised and pumped up by an emotional and motivated entomologist who has been able to describe her genuine, naive and fatal passion for the Beatles of her generation.

---

1 Andrea G. Pinketts (1960–2018), award-winning Italian writer, journalist, scriptwriter and TV personality.

2 *Here you go*

There is a difference, though. My favourite dish is the adolescence of a person who is ready and able to stew it in the pot of literature. Luisa Cartei is not a sixteen-year-old in love with some pretty boy named Gary Barlow. She is a premenstrual writer, and then, finally, a menstruated writer, hence bipolar. The young Alice hasn't had her first period yet, unlike the author, therefore she feels excluded from the circle (or circus) of her peers. She has no tits, just a hint of breast, and she is protected by a Kevlar sense of humour. Like a Mark Twain character, she ventures in her mother's wardrobe, among the dangers of reinforced bras and leopard print leggings.

Luisa Cartei, I have learned, is a blogger. She is not an influencer. She is a real writer, who can talk about flu or menstruation, like Stephen King in *Carrie*, or the fear of running out of gas like in *Christine*. The anxiety about her first kiss, which is "diabolically" procrastinated, and the fact that her father (the oncologist … damned cancer) forces her to distribute dinosaur-shaped stickers for cancer prevention outside her school make her a real hero. She is capable of saying "'Hey guys, would you like a free sticker?' I had never felt so dorky. Like Giorgio Mastrota on mattress commercials on TV; there's nothing worse than smart people who know they're doing an extremely stupid thing."

Among weekly publications like *Oggi* and *Cioè*, in Luisa Cartei's book the sketches become portraits and vice versa. Maybe someday I will even introduce her to Giorgio Mastrota, who's a dear friend of mine, and who, I'm sure, agrees with the author's way of thinking.

In conclusion, this is a syntonic, gin-and-tonic novel for those who, like me, have never had painful period cramps; and it is a liberty novel for those who have read *Isis Unveiled* by Helena P. Blavatsky or listened to *Finalmente Tu – Finally You* by Rosario Fiorello. And it's not an end …

# CHAPTER 1

# 1993

It was summer 1993. I was 15 years old and still had not become a "signorina", as my grandmother used to say, which meant that I hadn't had my first period yet, and that I had no boobs. Mine was a family of doctors, a family that took care of my girlhood in a clinical way. I had undergone several ultrasound scans and gynaecological examinations in order to establish whether I was normal, since all the girls of my age had had their period already and developed, like Kodak rolls turned into photographs of beautiful women.

At the end of the school year, my parents had sent me to Pisa, where my grandmother lived, hoping that the Tuscan air would have the same effect on me that it has on tomatoes, which are "riper and more savoury down there." They had been preparing for months for the arrival of the red river that would impetuously carry me into maturity, like the Arno River carries away rats and debris. They had booked the cake, bought the candles, put the invitations in an envelope and imagined the congratulations they would receive at the "I am a signorina" party. So, when I was 15, I was anxious to become a woman too.

Every month, a different gynaecologist ventured inside me like a miner with a flashlight on his helmet, searching for the hidden spring of maturity. I was still unripe, though, and being unripe had become a shameful flaw for me.

"Everything is OK," the gynaecologist kept repeating to my grandmother, Nonna Tilda, with her face between my thighs.

"I can't see anything here yet, but the menstruation will come, sooner or later." She had the husky voice of a smoker. She wore a magnifying glass on her right eye and looked like Sherlock Holmes into the maze of my vaginal canal. I was there, lying on the examination table with my legs open, waiting for the umpteenth verdict on my forthcoming womanhood. Some clinical terms were fascinating. "Will come." Menstruation will come? I didn't know whether to be amused or afraid. Would it look like zombies from *Thriller* or bleeding beefsteaks thrown by a sling? How would it come? How long would it stop by for? How would we introduce ourselves? Would it be polite or indiscreet? It was a strange feeling. I felt it as part of me, but at the same time as a stranger.

On the way home, it was always the same story. Nonna tried to comfort me with arrows of unintentional cruelty. "The hair has grown, that's a good sign. But the breasts are still tiny though …"

"Nonna, stop it! Can you lower your voice, please?" I begged her not to let all the people on the bus know how undeveloped I was, but she kept joking with her Tuscan irony.

"You will never be a busty woman, that's for sure! But you can always use padded bras or have plastic surgery!" Then, she burst out laughing and I felt pervaded by a sense of existential inadequacy.

Every year I used to spend the month of June at Nonna Tilda's house in San Benedetto, a district of San Frediano a Settimo, municipality of Cascina, in the suburbs of Pisa, Tuscany, Italy. I recall the list in this precise order because Nonna Tilda made me write about 57 postcards a year, to be sent to our relatives in Boston, Sydney and Rio de Janeiro. They were all descendants of the Innocenti family, whose names and faces my grandmother could barely remember.

"One day, you might need them," she used to say.

She had been having an epistolary relationship with an international network for years. Her network included:

» Jewish families she had hidden in her attic during the Second World War;

» university classmates who had studied paediatrics with her before moving to Calabria;

» general culture magazines, with which she had a real obsession.

She was the *Reader's Digest's* oldest subscriber, and she often sent me article clippings that she thought I would enjoy reading, with some comment attached. For example, "Washing your hair too much is bad for you." On that occasion, in addition to her comment, she had attached a braid made of her own hair, which dated back to the post-war period. It was chopped off, antique, creepy. With a note: "I used to wash it once a month, and yet look what nice hair I had when I was young!"

Staying with Nonna Tilda was also fun. These were my favourite activities:

» going with her to Rosa's pastry shop, where we used to buy 12 small cream cannoli, 5 of which ended up under Nonna's mattress. She ate them in secret, except the cream smudged around her mouth gave it away every time;

» spending entire sunny afternoons in the attic, searching for old toys;

» getting her to clap for me during my tennis lessons. Despite the burning afternoon sun, she could always find the strength to smile and to cheer me on;

» convincing her to give me 50,000 lire;

» persuading her to let me use her kitchen for my disastrous culinary experiments, including my famous raw-rice rice pie;

» challenging her to pick me up in her arms.

This last one was my favourite. At bedtime, Nonna used to carry me from the living room to my bedroom, by wrapping me up in a woollen flowered blanket. She would bend over me, close her eyes to concentrate and lift me up with all the strength she had in her tiny, thin, Audrey Hepburn body. During the journey, I could smell the scent of her elderly skin mixed with her sugary Chanel perfume.

The last time she was able to pick me up I was 9. As I grew up, she became smaller and smaller. She weighed 6 stones and was only 4 ft 10. A petite old lady; still, I felt safe with my arms around her. Little did I know how much I would miss those few inches of neck.

That day, as a prize for undergoing the umpteenth gynaecological examination, she allowed me to go out by myself. The album *Freak* (a name I identified with), by Samuele Bersani, had just been released, and the singer was launching it at the Feltrinelli bookstore in Pisa at 4p.m. It was an extraordinary event in that wasteland of desolate tediousness. Carmela was coming to pick me up. She was a summer friend, one of those friends I used to meet once a year, when I went from Northern Italy to Tuscany to spend the holidays at Nonna Tilda's.

My grandmother had been the most popular paediatrician in town and Carmela's parents were simple farmers. But she was my age, and her parents had forced her to keep me company during my weeks in Tuscany. Suddenly, all the social barriers had fallen. Nonna often had a doorway chat with the farmers, who told everybody that Doctor Innocenti was a dear friend of theirs. Nevertheless, they were still tomato producers to her.

Carmela came with her 18-year-old brother, Ruggero. "Get in the backseat. If the police stop us, I'm fucked," Ruggero welcomed us aboard his rusty red Seicento. He had just got his driving license. He was a handsome boy, even though his nails were constantly covered with hen shit. He was a farmer and collected eggs in his chicken coop every morning. And in the following 10 hours, his hands would never come across a bar of soap.

I liked Ruggero, but I avoided every thought regarding a possible relationship. I felt transparent, asexual, childish, innocent, like my surname, 'Innocenti', and dazed, like my namesake, 'Alice'.

I was aware that I was flat-chested, that my nails were too short and that I had a boring baby face. I was unaware that I had pretty green cat eyes and long, shiny blonde hair. In another context, I could have been quite attractive, but my context never changed: clip-on earrings, Barbie backpack, floral circle skirts, white socks and Velcro trainers. That was the result of a fitness-addicted mother and a daughter devoid of any spirit of rebellion.

"You have a driving license, don't you? We can sit wherever we like. We are not children, you idiot." Unlike me, Carmela was right in the middle of her hormonal-protest phase.

"I do, but you two are minors. I don't want to run the risk. I just got my license and I still don't know the rules, OK? So shut up and get in the backseat. Let me listen to Bersani!" We did as he said; after all, we didn't care about Bersani. We squeezed in the backseat, our heads together, to listen to the Walkman. With the windows down, we breathed in the smell of the summer in Tuscany, made of fresh rain, citrus fruits and freshly baked focaccia. At every red light, a different fragrance entered the car, replacing the chicken stink coming from Ruggero.

The most unforgettable scent, that day, was the sweet perfume of a fat woman with an orange scarf, who came up beside us on her moped. It reminded me of those tiny bottles of cheap perfume that one could find inside Easter eggs in the 1980s. It perfectly reflected my idea of Tuscany: simple, modest and slightly old-fashioned. Carmela protested against her brother, who had raised the volume to listen to *Chicco e Spillo,* in view of his meeting with the depressed singer from Romagna.

"Turn the fucking volume down!" Carmela was a "fuck" type of girl. Every time she said "fuck", she turned into an older, experienced, woman of the world, embittered by life. She scared me, but at the same time, she instilled a sense of respect. Maybe you were only allowed to say "fuck" if you had had your period. I was sure that Carmela had already had her first period, even if we had never talked about it. It was self-evident. She was tall, had big boobs, pimples on her forehead, stinky armpits, and she talked about boys. And, actually, she looked like a boy herself. She had short hair, she was as tall as her brother and had a deep voice. There was no hope for her anymore. She had developed into a bad photograph. Or maybe she had turned into a man. Carmela used her Walkman with her chubby fingers and stuck the headphone inside my ear every time it slipped out, that is, at every pothole in the road. "Listen to this. It's an English band. I recorded the song from Radio Dimensione Arno."

It was right there, in the backseat of a rusty red Seicento, on the route between San Frediano and Pisa Centrale, in a genuine and proletarian province, area code 050, when people still recorded songs from the radio on cassettes – whose tapes always twisted – that I listened to a song from my future favourite band, for the very first time. I never saw Carmela again, but I still remember us. I was 15, I still hadn't had my first period, and my farmer friend's Walkman played *Everything Changes*. And from that moment on, everything changed.

# CHAPTER 2

## My Mother

"Bullshit! One of these days, I'll rip up all these posters. This is your father's fault, he shouldn't be so indulgent. Quit listening to those 5 overpaid dancers and start studying."

School had just gone back, and the tiger of Bengal had started to yell at me all the time, as predictable as 10 years before, when her nails were sharper and polished in red, and her hands were more 1980s, just like her shoulder pads.

In the 1990s, her claws were round and smooth, her muzzle had turned into a sweet old face, her fur had become a pair of discoloured, spotted leggings and the tiger, all in all, was no longer so fearsome. However, my mother had been a legendary tiger.

I could have had an elephant mum, a fat homemaker who cooks stews and roasted pork, who makes lasagne while watching Gerry Scotti on TV and buys Dash detergent because "It Cleans Better." I could have had a fish mum, skinny, small, with dry blonde hair and pale skin- maybe an office worker or a secretary- one of those who get married young and have no ambitions. A mum with a gormless look, always there for you, but almost invisible, like wallpaper, a kind of peaceful species, friendly but not intrusive.

No, she was none of this; she was a tiger, a roaring tiger that imposed her rules and her life on the rest of the world. Among other things, just like a tiger, my mother could run for miles every day. She could have gone to Stockholm and back within 24 hours.

On her exercise bike, she could ride 500 miles at top speed and at the highest resistance level, with the most intense weight loss program. She used to get back home at midday, opening the door so vigorously that it would start vibrating; she would stop at the entrance of the hallway that led to my room and, if she sensed that nobody was around, she would move forward towards the bathroom, cautiously. She used to sigh rhythmically out of general disappointment, and at the same time, she would remove the picturesque armour that she had worn during her morning travels:

» my grandfather's old, artificial leather cross-country shoes;

» purple and silver Rambo headband;

» the diving suit she had bought by mistake, which was creased on one side (shark bite);

» the double wool socks bought at the Val di Fassa Alpini Festival.

As she got undressed, revealing her muscular body, her breath grew heavier and angrier. There was never a logic to her anger, but for some strange reason, on the route from Sweden to Italy, her sighs progressively filled with hatred toward the rest of the world, as if at every glance she could notice some kind of defect in the universe.

Once out of her travel clothes, she used to take off the sweat-inducing supermarket plastic bags she had wrapped around her calves, thighs, belly and chest. Then, naked, she would sit down on the edge of the tub with her legs half-closed and, leaning towards the bathroom sink, she would empty the plastic bags. From my bedroom, I could hear the noise of sweat being poured into the tub. In the meantime, two floors downstairs, my father would place his stethoscope between the folds of an elderly cancer patient's breasts, and coldly tell her that she had two months left to live.

It was in this context that I felt the need to fall in love with Gary Barlow. Of course, my mother disagreed and would brush everything and everybody off using her existentialist slogan: "Bullshit!"

Every afternoon it was always the same story. My mother would come to my room to check that I hadn't hung a new poster of Gary on the blue diamond pattern wallpaper. She couldn't help it. She tormented whoever would disturb her unstable mental balance, which was based on a few, serious obsessions:

» neatness of the house;

» no footprints on the marble floors ('pecche' in Venetian dialect);

» scrupulously scheduled breakfasts and dinners;

» telephone off in the evening hours;

» lights off at 9:05 p.m.;

» no unnecessary visits, doorbells or phone calls;

» no people in the kitchen while she was cooking;

» no change in the apartment decoration, including the 1980s blue diamond patterned wallpaper.

Most of the time, I would let her talk. My father, who was my secret ally, had once taken me aside and had explained that Mamma, poor thing, wasn't completely sane and that we had to let her vent. We had to consider her clinically sick. He used to say that she was a good woman and that he had sacrificed his life for her.

"Unfortunately," he used to add afterwards. My father and I were the smart ones, the chosen ones; therefore, we had to hold up.

My mother had had a tough life. She went to a boarding school in Switzerland when she was a child. Mean, sexually frustrated nuns forced her to eat meat, even though she was a vegetarian, and whipped her hands when she wouldn't behave. She was the youngest of 7 siblings. Three of them had died tragically. One was hit by a lorry, one had killed himself, and another one had

had a heart attack. She had contracted typhus when she was 20 and almost died. They had saved her by bringing her the penicillin by helicopter, just because she was rich. Every time I wanted to reproach my mother, I would think of all her existential pain, so I held back. I used to imagine her as a walking packet of calamity. She didn't know that, but even when I watched her stir the risotto, what I saw was a heap of past tragedies and clinical consequences. Perhaps I was influenced by my father's medical attitude.

It was curious how the tragedies she had experienced had affected her outfit. She had been wearing leopard print leggings and jumpers – without a bra – for 15 years. She was a fitness addict and the rest of the world seemed to her like an endless expanse of fat human beings. Unless you were anorexic, you would be obese to my mother.

"What do you want me to say? He is fat. If you only liked the dancer!"

"Do you mean Jason Orange, Mamma?"

"Yes, that one. Jacob Homage … at least he exercises."

"I love Gary for what he is, not for his appearance. He is the brains of the band, Mamma, and the soul of their songs. He is the poet of music. Plus, Jason has acne."

"What is that supposed to mean? I had acne too when I was young. And look at my perfect complexion now! Time to study, you have an oral test tomorrow."

"I have gym class and religion tomorrow. Relax."

After her daily "good parent" performance, my mother would close my bedroom's door and would go back to focus on her own life, as she had been doing perfectly for the last 45 years.

She had never tried to understand me; she had never played with me. She had never even knelt down to talk to me face to face when my height required it. She had never let me sleep in her bed and she had never hugged me. In general, since I was born, my mother had just tolerated me. That was her job, she used to say. She had had me to please my father, and now she couldn't back out.

I wasn't angry, though. That was my only reality. When I was sick, she would place her cool lips on my forehead to take my temperature, and I used to pretend that she was kissing me. In the afternoon, she would let me watch TV with her and she would make me some delicious ham and cheese sandwiches, together with a glass of cold milk. At the end of the day, in her own way, she loved me very much.

# CHAPTER 3

## Gary

I wasn't happy. But my life was objectively complete. Therefore, if I couldn't be happy back then, I might never have been.

I didn't hate my school, the Liceo Scientifico Newton. My marks were quite high. Math was a disaster, but I wrote decent essays and my English was good. I had a traditional family. My father was a doctor, and I admired him. I had a mother, whom I pretended to hate, and I had a grandmother, whom I adored. I had a nice home, a fancy 200 square-metre apartment on the river shore, in the city centre. I had a bitchy and spoilt best friend, who lived across the street, and 32 schoolmates, more or less stinky, more or less fun, more or less important in my underdeveloped-teenage life. And I had love. A man who, from the fixity of the poster, could never hurt me. What he could do was smile at me, or talk to me silently, through his eyes.

"How are you today, Alice?"

"Oh, that pullover suits you well, Alice!"

"Your hair is beautiful, Alice!"

"It's cold outside, Alice. Put something warm on!"

He was someone who could admire me like a mirror reflecting only my best side, ignoring my flaws, my insecurity and, above all, my immaturity.

It had all started after I listened to *Everything Changes* for the first time. I had spent the whole summer under the spell of a superior force, a spiritual calling to change my life. I had started with my stereo: no more Michael Jackson or Madonna. Only Take That. It was like a drug: *Pray, Love Ain't Here Anymore, Babe, It Only Takes A Minute*. I had bought all of their albums. In a couple of months, I had become addicted. The first time I saw them was on MTV. In *Everything Changes*, they were all dressed in elegant white suits. With hindsight, they actually looked like waiters at a South American wedding banquet in the 1970s. Nevertheless, they were undoubtedly handsome, and, most importantly, different from one another. You could choose between the black-haired, green-eyed one, the blonde-haired, blue-eyed one, the tall one, the fat one, the thin one, the athletic one, the funny one. To each her own.

First, I had chosen Mark, but there was too much competition, so I had fallen in love with Gary, the *fat one*. I liked the songs, but that was not the point. That was never the point for us fans. The point was that each one of us was deeply, viscerally, incontrovertibly sure that she would marry one of them. It would have been mathematically impossible, we knew that, and we felt sorry for all the others. Every fan knew, in the bottom of her heart, that she was the right one. Every Take That fan loved her Gary, her Robbie or her Mark wholeheartedly, and she never loved the same way again for the rest of her life.

During the day, I used to talk to Gary; at night, I would count the posters to fall asleep. Starting from the door anticlockwise, there were:

» the poster with bare-chested, platinum blonde, covered in hair gel Gary, from the *Do What You Like* video;

» the one with Gary wearing a red velvet suit and devil horns while singing *Relight My Fire*;

» the black and white one with Gary leaning against the wall staring at the horizon;

» the one with Gary on the stage, before a multitude of fans, wearing an electric blue suit and a black tie, with the microphone in his hand and the sweat running down his face, next to his earpiece (I could almost smell him: a blissful smell, like a biscuit dunked in milk … I would have liked to undress him and wash him slowly, touching him gently with the tips of my fingers in the shower);

» the close-up of Gary (his eyes were full of sensitivity, his soul was beautiful, sweet, honest, it was clearly visible in that photo: his skin looked like porcelain – perhaps they had retouched it – his lips were fleshy, half-closed, in an uncertain smile … maybe he wondered if he would ever find me.)

All those posters showed one clear thing; Gary wanted to be loved. He wanted someone who really understood him, beyond the celebrity and the spotlights. He wanted someone to hold at night under the quilt, someone to make love to in front of a fireplace, someone to share a house, a dog and holidays with. I knew I was that someone, his soulmate. I just needed to meet him, and he would recognise me. Before going to sleep, I always said goodnight to those posters. They were my confidants; they spoke to me.

"I want to hold you tonight, baby!" When I read those words in Gary's eyes, my hormones would blow up. A fire between my legs made me want to touch myself. I used to do it in the shower while thinking of him, of his kisses, of his caresses. But then I would stop. At church we had been taught that doing such things was a mortal sin. We would have gone to Hell. The dead watched us through the door. It was strictly forbidden. As soon as my fingers touched between my thighs, I would see the ghost of my late grandfather Sergio, staring at me. I would have been forced to touch myself with a sheet over my head for the rest of my life. Plus, I was afraid that I might never become a signorina. By touching myself down there, I could have damaged something and the process would terminate.

I wasn't living in the Middle Ages, but in a Catholic family, the topic of masturbation was dealt with in a medieval way, and the information remained buried under general embarrassment.

When I was home alone, I used to stage our encounters. I would plunder my mother's wardrobe and I would steal her silver sheath dress, fishnet tights and high-heeled shoes. I would stuff the corset with socks, put on mascara, eyeliner and red lipstick, and then we would start chatting.

I staged different situations. Sometimes, I was the girlfriend who had come to watch one of his concerts, some other times I was his lustful secretary. There were kisses, fights, marriage proposals. I knew I was crazy, but I was convinced that craziness was essential in a love relationship, so I didn't care too much.

"What are you doing, Alice?" Only once my father caught me red-handed, bursting into my bedroom hours earlier than usual.

"Just trying on some dresses for Matilda's party." Was it credible that my mother's silver sheath dress and the red lipstick were suitable for a 15-year old teenage party?

"You look like a prostitute. I prefer the polka-dot dress that Nonna Tilda gave you."

No, it was not credible.

My father, however, wasn't perturbed; maybe he didn't even understand.

"I'll go back downstairs."

"Bye, Papà."

He disappeared behind the door, with a snide smile on his face, peeked back into the room and added, "Who are you dressing like that for? The Swiss Milker?" He did understand.

"The Swiss Milker" was the nickname that my father had coined for Gary. He was blond, chubby and "rosy-cheeked", features that, according to my father, were typical of Swiss-German farmers. He had met many of them when he lived in Zurich and used to spend the weekends in the mountains. Milkers used to sit mainly on small wooden stools, milking cows into metal buckets. They wore Tyrolese clothes, laughed all the time and smelled like goulash and alcohol. "If you go there, you will find a thousand boys like him," then he added, "even better than him."

Once I finished my Indian ink shadows projection drawing and the last chapter on Italian medieval art, I could finally throw myself into my *Cioè* magazine; "Find out how Gary used to dress at 15."

# CHAPTER 4

## Tommaso

At some point my skinny, flared Levi's 495 were walking by themselves. From the moment Broncolato told me that they made my butt looked "great", I had started wearing them every day, for the whole 275 school days. They also never got washed: I was terrified at the idea of them shrinking or loosening up and therefore spoiling my only chance to be noticed by my second great passion: Tommaso Orpali.

When I wasn't thinking of Gary, I would think of Tommi. The difference was that Tommaso was real. He could talk to me, look at me, laugh at me. He could see how uncool I was. He made me nervous. He was one of those boys who had learned to only notice their philosophy Professor and the busty female schoolmates. He felt superior to the rest of the world; he had "boss' son syndrome": he had been allocated to the warehouse for work experience, already knowing he would become the general manager. He behaved as if his bright destiny was already set and, at the same time, he made the effort to talk politely to us, poor, nameless 'warehouse workers'; yet nobody had the privilege to enter his house.

*His house.* I imagined it to have comforting rooms, each with its own name on the door: 'Patience', 'Loyalty', 'Strength', 'Passion.' All those qualities were clearly reflected by the way he walked, the way he calmly put his books in his backpack, the way he sped on his white Vespa, like Prince Charming on his horse. I felt that I could have had a great life in that house.

Tommaso was in his third year in section A, only one year ahead of me, and he was out of reach, almost as much as Gary was. The queue of girls at his door was longer than the one at my first Take That concert. Only one time did he notice my existence and talked to me. He asked me where he could find the headband with the frogs that I was wearing. He wanted to buy one for his 10 year old cousin. I wanted to bury myself. I started mumbling "... it is not mine, actually ... I found it on the floor ... but, hey ... look ... I can give it to you. I prefer to wear my hair loose!"

He burst out laughing, pretending to buy my pathetic explanation. He accepted the headband because he would have felt embarrassed for me if he hadn't. After that day, I began to wear my hair loose and over my eyes. I looked like Jesus, with my hair parted in the middle, like theatre curtains hanging down my face. It was unbelievably straight. Perms and curlers were useless.

So, my Candy Candy style had turned into a Bee Gees style. Now I would walk along the school corridors with my crumpled, flared jeans and a blonde draw curtain almost always closed over my face.

I didn't even wash that often; I was certain that nobody would have ever ventured under my armpits. Hoping for potential kisses, though, I regularly brushed my teeth. However, for Matilda's party I got cleaned up. She was my best friend and the worst spoilt brat in the high school. We had grown up together.

I had gone to the hairdresser to get my first highlights done, then to the beauticians for the blackheads and finally I had searched in my mother's wardrobe to find something to wear that wasn't a pair of leggings.

It was as if my mother had got stuck in a department store in 1985. They had switched off the lights, closed the doors and left her in there, among fluorescent spandex pants, padded-shoulder jackets, high-waist jeans, exercise bikes and sweatbands. Even after her release and her return to modern society, she carried on wearing the same style. For this reason, finding a dress which was appropriate for a 15-year-old teenagers' party in 1993 was not easy at all. The best I could find, in fact, was green viscose leggings, a black shoulder-padded bodysuit and a pair of Tod's ankle boots.

"You look so gaunt. It's not good. It's clear that you are still a little girl," observed my mother. "I've got an idea though!". She started adding layers to my clothes, just to make me curvier.

"Put those two pairs of woollen socks under your leggings! They will give you thickness, adding at least two centimetres!" My mother exulted. "Tricks of the trade!" she said winking at me.

"What trade?" I asked, "You have never worked in your whole life!"

"It's an expression. You are always so critical," she said, disappointed.

"OK, but I'm melting in here!" I complained. Summer had just ended, and the temperature was still semitropical. Once dressed, as I was heading to the door, I heard her yelling. "Wait! Come here!" She was running after me along the corridor waving a pad of hers. "Put it in your pants!". She added. "It will be visible through the leggings and people will think that you have your period."

I snorted, looking at the floor with the same sad look of a dog that has to be muzzled before going out. "We don't want them to think that you're different, do we?" she specified thoughtfully. So, as stuffed as a turkey on Christmas Day and gripped by cold sweat, when I got to the Marchettis' front door, I had already lost 85 percent of my dignity and 99 percent of my body fluids. When Matilda made her first comment on my appearance, I lost the last percentage left of hope for the night.

"You are pitiful." That was her first reaction. Then she added, "You're going to embarrass me dressed like that at my party." It was clear that my mother's tricks of the trade had not performed miracles on me, or maybe Matilda's trade was different from my mother's. In the following 30 minutes, I underwent an extreme makeover, like the doll with platinum blonde hair which I used to put make up on, comb and ravage when I was a little girl.

Alessia, Matilda's elder sister, gave me one of her bras, and then she stuffed it with 10 little multicolour cotton balls – very trendy at the time – yellow, blue, white and pink. As for the size, I switched from a double A to a double D in a few seconds: little miracles of the Teen Age. In my opinion, the tight bodysuit made the whole thing look blatantly artificial. Matilda and her sister, however, reassured me. "Don't be paranoid, you look great. As long as nobody touches you … which, of course, will never happen!" Then they burst out laughing. They put make up on me, gave me their mother's high-heeled shoes and clip on earrings – since I didn't have my ears pierced. (Another clear sign of my "artificiality" and hormonal immaturity.) I felt like the young Shirley Temple when she played adult roles. A fake.

The doorbell started ringing continuously and guests started to arrive. Girls got super-excited, as they saw the boys coming in, all you could hear was hysterical cries and the noise of inexperienced heels on the parquet floor. As far as I was concerned, boys were terrifying. Maybe it was an ovarian-age issue.

"Hey Tommi! Fourth floor!" As Matilda said those words over the intercom, I stopped breathing.

*Tommaso Orpali?* Fear. Terror. Paralysis. I couldn't believe it. What was Tommaso Orpali doing at Matilda's birthday party?

"It's Tommi. I didn't think he would come. He said that he had nothing better to do!" declared Matilda, arousing a collective agitation. Some girls rushed to fix their makeup, some went to the toilet, a few had a gin and tonic. All of this happened during the 100 seconds that it took him to reach the fourth floor from the building's front door. I was dripping with sweat and could barely move, as a result of the unstable architecture of my clothes. With every step I took, I felt the little balls in my bra moving away from their original position. From the outside, one could have seen my boobs changing their shape over and over again, depending on the way those little cotton balls moved around the bra, first lumpy strawberries, then deformed potatoes.

"Damned fake tits!" I kept repeating to myself.

"What did you say?" Broncolato showed up out of nowhere behind me with a glass of Fanta.

"Damned fake cigs!" I answered promptly. "I was thinking that they should invent them, so that people could smoke with no health risk!". And I pointed at the Murano vase where Matilda's parents kept their Merit cigarettes and the cigars.

Broncolato ignored my concern about the good for humanity. "No jeans today?" he asked maliciously.

"No, my mother's leggings today. They are more elegant, aren't they?" I answered.

"Too bad … those jeans … you know …" He continued.

"… Make my butt look great, yes I know."

"Well, at least you have tits today," he concluded, staring at my lumpy strawberries. I wanted to bury myself. Did he notice? Was it obvious that they were fake? Then he added "G.P.F.F. (Good Prospects For the Future) … if they keep on growing like that, I'm going to marry you in a few years."

"Idiot!" I blushed. No, he didn't notice the artificiality of my asymmetrical breasts. After all, his judgment was not reliable. Broncolato was an absent-minded beanpole. And he had never kissed a girl, so he probably didn't even know what real boobs looked like.

Tommaso had entered the room. My hands, closed around a glass of Schweppes, began to shake in Parkinson's disease mode. He was greeting everyone charmingly. He was at ease. After all, he didn't know anyone there, but everybody knew him. If I were him, I would have felt the same way. And I would have been even more at ease, if I hadn't seen him coming my way. Straight towards me, through the crowd, like Moses crossing the Red Sea. Inexorable, he raised his arm, and I feared he wanted to touch my fake breasts to unmask me in front of all those people.

"We don't know each other. I'm Tommaso. Nice to meet you." As he stretched his hand to shake mine, I replied automatically, "Alice. Nice to meet you too." I didn't know whether to feel relieved because he hadn't touched my cotton-ball breasts, or humiliated because he had totally forgotten that we knew each other, that we had already spoken and that I had walked near him every morning at school during the last year. I had even given him my headband, and still he didn't recognise me. I was overwhelmed by humiliation and discouragement. My boobs were misshapen; I felt a little ball slip under my right armpit.

I had sunk into Matilda's father's zebu leather armchair, and Broncolato had begun to torment me with his endless and boring arguments while sipping soft drinks. Probably, he had assumed I was his best prospect for the night.

Tommi disappeared among the girls with real tits, those wearing perfume and tampons. Matilda had disappeared with Vittorio up the blue winding staircase. I wondered if they were making out or making a baby. After them, other girls and boys would climb those stairs: Mascia, Viviana and Eleonora with Marco, Nicola and Mattia. The winding staircase was made for those who were able and wanted to smooch. Usually, the boy asked the girl, "Do you want to get off with me?" and, if she nodded, they would go upstairs to the paradise of pleasure.

I had never been there. At least, not with a boy. Just with Matilda to watch cartoons. Upstairs there was Matilda's father cinema room, illegally built using a part of the attic and furnished with all sorts of amenities: a very comfortable sofa with a grey flannel cover, a huge TV, soft lights and a sound system imported from America, that covered the whole wall. When there was a party, they disconnected the sound system from the TV and used it as a music speaker. Usually, it was Alessia, Matilda's sister, who would choose the music, and she always selected Jovanotti.

That night, miraculously, Alessia chose Take That. *Love Ain't Here Anymore*, a masterpiece of romantic pop music. "You can hear the gloomy notes, the half-tones, the F-sharp … this song makes you dream." Before I knew it, I had started teaching a class on Take That. The boys looked amused. The girls were intrigued.

"Are you the girl who knows everything there is to know about Take That?" Out of the blue, Tommaso Orpali spoke to me again.

"Yes, I have met them in person." I answered. At that point I became trapped in my lie, just like the cotton ball in my bra. I added, "I have been to London and I met them outside their hotel." Another lie. "I'm in touch with Gary. We are friends." I was a factory of lies.

"Hey, I know you. You are the headband girl, aren't you?" Tommaso suddenly changed the subject.

The headband girl. I was the headband girl. Nothing more. My existence was defined by a plastic, circular, upholstered thing. This is what I was in his world.

"I guess so," I replied. Because actually I wasn't sure anymore whether I was the headband girl or the cotton ball girl – another shape defining who I was.

"I'm so sorry. How embarrassing! I introduced myself again earlier," he justified himself.

Coolly I replied: "No problem! I do that all the time. I have such a bad memory. I hadn't recognised you." I was a listed holding company of lies.

"The reason is that you have changed. You look better with loose hair. You should always wear it like that." Tommi had just said that he liked something about me, or maybe it was about my shape.

So, just like I had done with my jeans, I decided that I would never change the colour, length, shampoo or style of my silky blonde hair again.

"Would you like to go upstairs?" he asked me.

The universe stopped. My heart began to pound as if it was about to explode. Tommaso Orpali had asked me, just me, to go up the winding staircase. I panicked. He didn't know that I wasn't a woman yet. That my boobs were made of messy cotton. That my legs were stuffed with socks. That inside my pants there was an armour of unused pads. That I was completely and pathetically fake, from head to foot.

I imagined his hands slipping underneath my viscose bodysuit, while my teeth clumsily bumped his as I tried to give him my very first kiss. I imagined Tommaso bursting out laughing and myself crying. I imagined that I would no longer be the headband girl, but the fake tits girl, the loser who can't kiss a boy.

Looking at the floor, with my cheeks blazing with embarrassment, I told him: "Sorry. I have to go. It's late. See you at school!"

In less than no time, I found myself rushing towards the door as I hurriedly said goodbye to my friends. I slid out the flat as quickly and noiselessly as an ice skater on her blades. It was a perfect exit. I was not there anymore, but nobody would remember the exact moment I left. I would always remember, though, Tommi's reaction: his deep and gentle look turned surprised first, then standoffish. He wasn't used to getting a 'no' as an answer. He had turned his back on me and had walked off before I could make a move. He hadn't even said goodbye. I still remember his wide shoulders, his tall and slim silhouette and his blue, cashmere polo neck as he headed to the kitchen.

As the lift was going down, I felt a raging frustration. My legs began to sweat under the woollen layers, my stomach was twisted regretting the missed chance, and I started to rip off my cuticles. My conscience reproached me. *Alice, for God's sake, grow some balls!*

When I stepped out of the lift, the cotton balls broke out of my bra and crushed all around my shoes.

And those were the only balls I had left.

# CHAPTER 5

## The Smurfs

If my father had been born evil, he would have become a serial killer; but, since he was a good man, he had restricted himself to being a serial driver. From 1984 to 1994, he bought 8 versions of the same car: Lancia Thema.

It was the only luxury he granted himself: cruising around Italy, like a corrupted politician, in his metallic-painted flagship vehicle, in an era where the concept of metallic paint was a luxury in itself. The colours of his cars changed over the years. Light green, light blue, light grey, light brown. Cream coloured alcantara suede interiors – which my mother defined as "Another bullshit of your father" – and cellophane covering the interior, as was normal in those days in Italy. My father was obsessed with that plastic upholstery, the one you could have found in new cars, which covered seats and doors. For 2 years, namely the whole period he kept the same car, nobody had the permission to remove the plastic. "I don't want the car to get ruined," he would say. I remember when we used to go to Calabria. It took 14 hours, and, sitting in the backseat, I pinched small pieces of plastic to let the seats get some air. "Don't touch it, or you will stain the alcantara suede." We would arrive at our destination soaked with sweat, but the car was still intact.

Thinking about it now, I am sure my father had a mental disorder.

» "Syndrome of Extreme Packaging"

» "Congenital Mental Plasticization"

» "Brain Cell(ophane) Cancer"

Maybe he was just afraid to reveal secrets. Or to show a weak spot. Maybe his subconscious tried to defend itself against the perils of life. Maybe my mother had worn him out over the years, and he couldn't take it anymore. Maybe he used prostitutes and he wanted to safeguard the seats. Maybe he didn't want his fragile soul to be touched because he didn't want to suffer. Maybe he was just a psycho.

Anyway, while pinching that plastic cover, I used to think of my situation: I was like the alcantara suede interiors. Virgin. I had proved it at Matilda's party. I was imprisoned in my own suffocating plastic cover, unable even to say yes to the prettiest boy in the school. Nobody would ever touch or stain me. I would be sad forever, like an unused car. Like Doctor Innocenti's metallic light blue Thema. When those thoughts crossed my mind, I felt the need to tear off that plastic more and more.

One day, on our way to Nonna Giannina's house in Bassano, I had torn off half of the back seat. Was it my parents' fault? Were they overprotective? Was it my fault? Why was I such a loser?

I thought how I would have liked to see those cream-coloured seats stained with blood. My blood. The day that I would have become a woman. A magnificent red flow that would have caused Papá a heart attack. But maybe becoming a woman depended on me as well. I had to rip that plastic apart. Blood would follow.

"Hey sweetheart, would you like to stop in Limena to buy a Smurf?" my father asked me. Every foggy and rainy autumn Sunday in the Po Valley – precisely 1225 times – between the 1980s and the 1990s, we used to go to visit Nonna Giannina, who lived near Bassano del Grappa. On the way back, my father used to buy me a Smurf at Bianchin's Newsagent. We had collected 190 Smurfs, including many versions of Azrael and Gargamel. This happened until I turned 15, when I began to collect Take That merchandise. However, I still had a soft spot for the Smurfs. And more than anyone else for my father, my Papa Smurf. He was the man I loved the most – even more than Gary – the man I kept deluding into thinking that he could take care of me as if I still were his little girl.

"OK, Papà. One last Smurf. If they have the pissed-off one, get that," I replied.

"Mind your language! A respectable young lady doesn't talk like that!" he reproached me as he was parking the car.

When he scolded me, he used to frown and rotate his eyes anticlockwise. After once around, I was forgiven.

"OK, I'll come with you," I said. Slamming the plasticized door, I accompanied my papá into Bianchin's. Bianchin's wasn't just a newsagent, he sold tobacco and toys as well, like most shop-keepers back then. He was a hybrid, like those women wearing padded shoulders who looked like American football players.

The tobacconist was a quiet man, in his sixties, with a white full beard. He reminded me of a forest ranger. (Don't ask me why.) He used to see us about 30 Sundays a year, but the most famil-iar greeting he could give was "Hello, Doctor, which Smurf are you going to buy today?"

That day, when we entered the shop, we found that the toys had been replaced with Take That posters and magazines. They were everywhere. Smurfs and Barbies had been relegated to a corner. Just when my father was about to choose the Smurf, I read something sensational. "Take That will sing at the Sanremo Music Festival."

My heart was bursting with excitement.

"Papà! Please! Drop the Smurf, let's buy this magazine!"

"Aren't you tired of those 4 rockers?"

"There are 5 of them and they play pop music …! Anyway no! I am not tired of them; I never will be …" I replied jumping up and down with excitement. "Please, please, please!" I said, trying one more time to convince him, with my hands clasped together and my 'I love you', sweet daddy look. My sweet papá put the Smurf away and bought the magazine with the bomb-shell news about Take That. He looked quite shocked.

"It's normal, doctor. Children grow up." Unusually, Mr Bianchin tried to start a conversation, looking at me paternally. I had the feeling that he was staring at my tits, as if he wanted to gather evidence that what he had just said was true.

Had I really grown up? Judging from his look I thought that he had changed his mind and wanted to go back to the Smurfs. I would never find out, because that was the last time I saw Mr Bianchin. I don't know whether he died shortly afterwards or whether he went to live in the woods. (Don't ask me why.)

I could never have imagined that my mother would have stored all my Smurfs in the basement that same evening, wrapped in plastic like my dad's car. That day, the Smurfs left my present and became part of my childhood, like our visits to Nonna Giannina and Mr Bianchin.

"What did you buy?" asked my mother threateningly as we got back in the car. It was not a question, but an expression of disapproval.

"Hold on. I have to read this," I answered. "Papá, try to drive properly for the next 10 kilometres."

"You can't talk to your father like that! Aren't you ashamed?" replied my mother as dad was putting his Sunday-driver gloves on.

"… and so, the British band, despite official denials, will allegedly be on the stage at the next Sanremo Music Festival," I read aloud for Papá Smurf.

"Yes, but it says allegedly. This is just bullshit made up by journalists. And you two, numbskulls, have taken the bait and bought that magazine," complained my mother.

"You can't talk to your husband like that, Mamma," I corrected her.

"What else does it say, Alice?" asked my father, pretending to be interested in order to avoid a sudden review of his marriage.

"Here it says that they might be staying in Nice. Which makes sense, if they are going to Sanremo …" I was in the middle of some creative brainstorming.

"Why don't they sleep in Sanremo, then?" my mother insisted.

"Honestly, Mamma. You know nothing about these things! Do you think that a celebrity would sleep and perform in the same place? I mean, do you eat where you sleep or drink coffee where you eat?" This last statement confused my mother a lot. I could play with words like a juggler with oranges. Before you realised that it was nonsense, it could even sound brilliant.

"I don't know … this world is crazy," she cut short. But then, the look upon her face changed. Maybe we had touched a sensitive, emotional subject. "Oh, Nice. What a good time we had there with Zia Esmeralda," my mother sighed.

I was right, then. Then came a story about my aunt Esmeralda, her sister.

"Zia Esmeralda and I were young and pretty. There were no immigrants around and everything was so expensive," she went on. (*Snobbish* and *racist* were two words that suited her like two diamond earrings.) "That was a fantastic holiday, Alice … you are such losers now, with all these ugly, poor and dangerous people. You have no idea … back in the days, Nice was frequented by Liz Taylor, Gregory Peck, Robert Redford."

"OK, Mamma," I tried to ignore her.

"That was the summer when miniskirts became fashionable. Do you remember that, Armando?"

Whenever she talked about fashion, sport or sex – especially sex – my mother was at peace with the world. Her eyes filled with tears, and nostalgia kidnapped her and took her to a place only she would know. Thank God.

She went on: "I had a *mini* miniskirt! No longer than a belt. We wore no pants. Beach parties were great! Everything was classier."

"I know, Mamma." I resigned to listening to her story.

She kept her eyes closed, as she was in the grip of an endless reminiscence. "I was super thin. I never ate, and, when I did, I puked straight away. I was tanned and I used to put lots of make up on. And we smoked, as cigarettes were not cancer-causing yet."

"Cigarettes have always been cancer-causing, Mamma," I corrected her.

"Yes, but we didn't know that then. So it didn't count. Like AIDS, the plague of your generation. You can't even enjoy a shag," she concluded.

"Mamma!" I reproached her, smiling.

Talking about sex with parents was embarrassing, like when there was an erotic scene on TV, and you watched it all together in the living room.

"Anyway, Nice is very close to Sanremo, not even an hour away. I remember when Zia Esmeralda and I ran away," she continued.

"Ran away from what?" I asked.

"Well yeah ... you know that Zio Tito, her first husband, had many enemies. On August 15th they blew up his yacht, on the harbour pier. They wanted to kill us, but they timed it wrong, we had gone to do the shopping."

Zio Tito had enemies? A yacht blew up? My mother with no pants? I was shocked. I always was when my mother told a new chapter of her biography. I didn't interrupt her.

"... We had gone to the harbour supermarket to buy oysters and champagne. Zio Tito had decided to get off the yacht because he needed to call his accountant. We were walking back down the pier ... his boat was the farthest. All of a sudden, the pier started shaking, it was like an earthquake, then the explosion, there was fire, smoke, people screaming. We didn't realise at first what had just happened. We thought of a kidnapping, a terrorist attack, an atomic bomb ... When we figured it out ... we were blown away, so to speak. Zio Tito ran back towards us, he told us to drop the oysters and the champagne, pulled us by the arms and we ran away."

"Mamma, how could you drop the oysters and the champagne?" I asked ironically.

Unfortunately, irony was not one of my mother's gifts, so she resumed her narration.

"Actually, you are right. Take That could easily sleep in Nice and perform in Sanremo. And anyway, those bastards managed to kill Zio Tito in the end." She concluded.

The Brenta mafia had killed Zio Tito two years after the explosion in Nice. He was in his house, in Vicenza. A masked man, who was never identified, had shot him four times.

So, with my mother's approval, I booked a room in Nice for 2 nights during the Sanremo Music Festival, in the same hotel where my mother and Liz Taylor used to sleep in the 1960s.

# CHAPTER 6

## Christmas

You knew it was Christmas when the doorbell never stopped ringing. Plants, trees, bunches of flowers, baskets full of exotic fruit and vegetables, paintings, Hermes bags, towel sets, jewellery, watches, Persian rugs; these were just some of the presents that my father used to receive during the holiday season from his recovered patients, those in treatment and even dead patients, I suppose. Every present had the most heartfelt thank-you or prayer messages attached.

» "Doctor, you are like God to us."

» "Doctor, we don't know how to thank you enough."

» "Doctor, we will never forget you."

» "Doctor, please make me live."

In some of them we were mentioned as well.

» "Give a hug to your family on our behalf."

» "Merry Christmas to you and to your women."

» "Thank you, doctor, thanks to your beautiful daughter and thanks to your amazing wife."

It was as if the more their cancer cells had decreased, the more they used sparkling adjectives. It was a kind of language-therapy. My father's patients did their best to choose redundant expressions and thrilling adjectives. I could almost distinguish the presents sent by the living patients from those sent by the dead ones, simply by counting the number of words on the cards.

That's how I grew up. I was used to hearing my father talking on the phone with people who would suddenly stop calling. I was used to heartfelt, desperate and resigned voices, which I learned to distinguish from one another. When I picked up the phone, I liked to listen to those voices. I felt that I had to calm them down. I still didn't understand death, but I had learned to understand life. I had learned to perceive the brevity of life. I knew that it could last the time of a conversation. I knew that life was like a phone call that one day you would no longer make.

Maybe that was the reason I used to live in a hurry. Always moving. My frenetic existence was in dark contrast to the routine in which my mother had found her raison d'etre. These Christmas intrusions began to bother her, after the first hour.

"I can't stand this doorbell anymore! We have to tell your father that this has to stop, I'm going to lose my mind. Why don't they deliver them to the hospital?" Then she lowered her eyes, and it almost seemed that she was going to say something loving to make amends. "Sometimes I think that it would almost be better if he hadn't saved so many patients, then I wouldn't have to polish all this silverware!"

I would let her talk, like a therapist who surrenders to the ravings of the patients lying on the couch.

"Within 10 days, we won't be able to walk in here anymore. The living room has become a mausoleum … And the kitchen is like a greenhouse … The tables are covered in useless knick-knacks and there's no space left. It's a nightmare!" All of a sudden, though, a smile of approval appeared on her face: "Except for the oranges, of course!"

Every year, one present outclassed all the others, always the same, and my parents waited for it with excitement: Mr De Mari's Sicilian oranges. Thanks to that juicy surprise, I had to eat oranges for 2 months in a row, and I inevitably got a permanent cold sore due to the excess of vitamin C.

"Oh, Mr De Mari's oranges!" My mother used to rush to the door so eagerly that I've always wondered whether she liked the oranges or Mr De Mari. I later found out that, during the 1970s, Mr De Mari had worked as Paul Newman's lookalike in Cinecittà, the Roman Hollywood. And maybe that was one of the reasons why my mother loved Sicilian oranges so much. "Anyway, thank God Mr De Mari has survived. It would have been a shame to see so much beauty die."

"Yes, Mamma," I replied as I walked out the door to go to school and as the doorbell was ringing for the first time that day. My mother sighed and I almost felt sorry for her. "I'll open when I get downstairs, Mamma. Have a good day."

As I walked, I imagined my mother completely covered by presents. I would find her suffocated among piles of wooden baskets, silver cups and orchid pots. I wondered if, in all the history of mankind, anyone had ever died smashed under Christmas presents. Maybe a lorry driver delivering Christmas hippopotamuses at the zoo. Maybe the homo habilis, crushed by wrapped rolling stones with Christmas cards attached.

I always imagined nonsense. The pictures in my mind took me away. If I lingered over a vision, this would develop into surreal scenes, into far and absurd spaces, where anything is possible. For example, when I stared at my posters, I "zoomed in" on Gary's eyes to find myself in Kenya, riding an elephant, and to find those very same eyes next to me, as Gary held me tight with a whip in his hand, wrapped in a golden sarong.

Maybe my mother also "zoomed in" on the Christmas presents to go back to relive her sweet memories of the first years of love with my father. Maybe she found herself in Sardinia again, dancing the cha-cha with a young, ambitious, tanned and passionate doctor – as she had always described him. Maybe she remembered what made her fall in love with him: his dedication to his job, his ambition to save the world. Maybe, in the twinkle of the silverware, she could see the faraway reflection of herself, when she was young, happy and affectionate. Maybe, going back to the reality of a home invaded by knick-knacks, she wondered what had happened to her, perhaps the same thing that had happened to our flat: she had been gradually suffocated by unwanted objects and responsibilities. *We don't need all these things. Things kill.* Maybe this is what my mother had thought.

# CHAPTER 7

## Laura

Laura and I had arranged to meet after school to outline our get-away plan. Sanremo was two months away, I had my mother's permission – my father's was not essential – and we needed to organise our encounter with Take That.

"We need to escape on Friday night, after dinner. I will have to go out with some excuse, without making any noise. My father has a shift at the hospital on Friday …" I was speculating as Laura chewed her Big Babol.

"What about your mother?" she asked.

"Mamma usually falls asleep after a bottle of prosecco. She shouldn't be a problem," I said giggling.

"I've checked the train timetables. We can leave at 9 p.m. and be in Nice at 6 a.m. the next morning. We could book two reclining seats. Forward-facing, otherwise I could feel sick."

"Do you seriously get train sick? You're strange."

"Didn't you know that already?" she replied, snapping her bubble gum.

"And then? How will we move around? Do we have any contacts?" I asked her.

"Of course we do! We need to get to the airport and wait for their flight from London to land. I have high-profile contacts in France!" She stressed "high-profile" raising her left index finger, as if she was teaching a lesson.

"What do you mean?" I asked intrigued.

"We have 3 contacts. A bouncer working at the ice-cream shop in the French Riviera, who is friend of my tailor. A Parisian taxi-driver, classmate of my neighbour's grandfather. And a German landlady who has given us a discount because usually she rents rooms on an hourly basis."

"We are in good hands then …" I replied sarcastically.

I wasn't the kind of girl to run away from home. Maybe if I had piercings, I would have been more credible. But with my baby face, my high grades and the fear of disappointing my parents, I doubted I could ever make it.

And I hadn't told Laura the truth. I wasn't running away from home. Not only were my parents happy for me to go, but they had also booked the hotel for us and so we didn't need to sleep in a pay-by-the-hour hotel. But I never told Laura. I was afraid that the truth would disappoint her, and she had been disappointed by the truth her whole life.

Laura and I had met on the 'Teletext', the 1990s' version of WhatsApp. It was a transcendental, surreal place, between a TV screen and the information board at the gate of Purgatory. Teletext was used mostly by:

»   deaf-mutes;

»   pensioners;

»   paedophiles;

»   Take That fans, who contributed to its greatest expansion in 1994.

By using the remote control for the subtitles for the deaf, you could access the Take That chat. Messages could be sent using the control buttons. If you asked me to do that today, it would be easier for me to get a degree in astrophysics. On the chat, you could briefly express your wishes, for instance "I love Gary and wanna have sex with him", "Gary's wife wants to go to London", "Gary is mine, fuck off", "Sanremo fan – call me". You could also add your nickname – mine was Garyswife – and leave your phone number, so that every paedophile or rapist on the planet could call you the next day; 1990s naivety.

I wasn't sure about which message to choose and so I had posted them all. Rigorously, in English, because we, the fans, already felt British by choice. As for the sexual allusions, it was just a way to seem older than we actually were. Most of us had never even kissed a boy.

This is how I had met Laura. She had answered my message, making it clear that she liked Robbie so we could be friends, or each other's maid of honour. We had found out that we were neighbours, we had thought that it was a sign of destiny and we had decided to meet in person the following Saturday afternoon in front of my school.

I still remember her, leaning against a column, under the porches of Via Dante, wearing her black overalls, with a cigarette in her hand, like a factory worker during her lunch break. Her maturity was summarised by her nose piercing. Her nose was thin and perfect. The piercing was an aquamarine brilliantine. It lit up her round and pretty face. Her sweet brown eyes were hardened by a men's haircut, with a blue lock that covered half her face.

She was a heap of womanliness wrapped in a male uniform, like Chinese children's feet wrapped so tight that they can't grow, or lesbians' breasts flattened under their clothes. She was 2 years older than me and she looked totally self-confident. She was completing a technical school, but she had failed a year – another indicator of sexual maturity.

She came from the suburbs and she was clearly more down-to-earth than me. A little bit like Carmela, her family was humble, so I knew we could get along because I had a certain influence on her. After all, I had spent the best moments of my life with country friends. Coarseness made me feel free. It was like moving to another world, a world far from mine, where nobody knew me, and I could walk down the streets with my pyjamas on. No one would have noticed me and, even so, I would have looked more elegant than them.

Laura had seen me coming from the distance, and we had immediately recognised each other. Before even shaking hands, we were blood sisters. That afternoon lasted forever. We chewed bubble gum for hours, bought an ice cream, walked on the cobblestones of the city squares, wore out our shoes and our jeans. We laughed, exchanged dreams and opinions, stumbled into angry and hurried people, daydreamed impossible plans without watching our step, while the melted ice cream trickled down our fingers; in other words, we were being teenagers.

We never took our eyes off each other. We were like two trains entering the station at the same time: looking at each other from the window, each of us with a different origin and background, perfectly synchronised and ready to get off at the same stop.

In our friendship, there was a sense of big discovery, anticipation, pure feeling. We knew we could never be parted. We shared an impossible dream, which we had to fulfil at any cost. After some brief small talk, our thoughts turned to a getaway plan.

Laura used to spend her holidays in Alassio, where, at the beach, she had met a distinguished man. He was the doorman of the Ariston, the theatre where the Sanremo Music Festival takes place. It had been a fair exchange: Laura's mother had granted him an autograph from her brother (Laura's uncle was the Genoa football club goalkeeper) and in return, the man had got her two tickets for the festival.

Of course, no Take That fan had ever watched the festival before, unless forced by their 85-year-old grandmother, in love with the host, Pippo Baudo.

That year everything changed. In January, Take That would be on the stage to release their new single, *Sure*. From that moment onwards, Sanremo became Saint Remo: our personal saint, our faith, our Lourdes. That year, one way or another, Sanremo had become our pilgrimage.

"Fourth row, left side, seats 22 and 23. If we are lucky, we will be on the side of the singers and not of the orchestra!" Laura proudly showed me the tickets. We would be almost able touch them, to throw our phone numbers at them, screwed up into paper balls, and they would call us to spend the night together. The following day, they would realise that they loved us. Maybe they would still have gone on tour. But we would have got pregnant and we would have told them. They would have realised that we were the perfect women for them, and we would have got married in a farm on the hill near Manchester. We could have had a double wedding, actually.

There would be horses, celebrities and all our schoolmates who doubted our abilities. I would have invited Tommaso Orpali, to make him realise what he had missed. And Matilda, just to see her green with envy.

Maybe, for the occasion, I would have had breast implants, so I wouldn't have needed cotton balls. My father would have hugged Gary and asked him permission to call him Swiss Milker. Gary would have lovingly accepted. My mother would have been elegant, for a change, wearing some famous designer's dress that I would have been able to afford. We would have lived happily ever after, making love and popping out babies. Gary would have looked me in the eyes every day of his life, telling me how much he loved me. We would have been beautiful, rich, famous and happy.

Our fantasy carried us dreamingly through that afternoon of naïve teenager-hood. Until I realised that there was something wrong with the whole story. I didn't menstruate. I couldn't get pregnant.

All of a sudden, the daydream took a turn for the worse: Laura would have lived her dream and I would have stayed in the background, watching her going away. Her train would have overtaken mine and we might never meet again.

That tragic thought, and the fact that it was 8 o'clock and it was late, interrupted our chat. Only afterwards, I realised that my hard luck was actually a big advantage. My parents would have let me live my life without opposing me. It wouldn't have mattered if I had slept with Gary or shared the train seat with a paedophile met on the teletext. One thing was definitely certain: I wouldn't have come home pregnant.

# CHAPTER 8

## School

*Summer of '69* by Bryan Adams was the perfect song to solve exponential equations to. I had also found out that John Coltrane's *Giant Steps* helped me easily memorize the vectorial system. What's more, I had entirely copied the lyrics of Mietta's *È Di Nuovo Gennaio* in an essay, getting a great mark. During the Christmas holidays something extraordinary had happened: I had listened to different music. Another 1990s miracle had occurred. That is, I had been fooled by one of those CD offers you could find in *Oggi* magazine. You could pick 5 CDs for free and they would deliver them within 5 days. Without obligation. Actually, there was an obligation at the bottom of the page, written in tiny letters. And the obligation implied that, once the bait was taken, further CDs would keep being delivered, at the price of 30,000 lire each. Forever.

The interesting thing was that you couldn't even choose the subsequent CDs. Some kind of music god would pick for you, with the aim of indoctrinating you, hypnotising you or making you the biggest owner of musical scraps of unsold stock.

As a result, during the holidays, I kept listening to extreme jazz, underground heavy metal and songs in the Neapolitan dialect; and, every now and then, some classic songs. Overall, later in life, this helped me solve Trivial Pursuit questions and make me appear like a sort of expert.

Basically, I owe my personal musical culture to *Oggi* subscriptions.

It was the first day of school after the Christmas holidays and I got there super prepared, as usual. Maths, Italian, English, Science, Chemistry, History of Art, Technical Drawing, Physics,

Religion. All my notebooks were perfectly aligned on my desk, ready to be handed in to the teachers.

I hadn't grown up at all and was there in the usual Levi's, worn to death, braids to conceal my dirty hair that I was too lazy to wash after the heavy lasagne dinner, psychedelic-pattern polo neck jumper and a pink and yellow Invicta schoolbag- a Christmas present from my favourite uncle, Zio Francesco, which came with a note; "You can't go to school with that shitty, pathetic Barbie thing anymore!"

But I had tried to grow up. I had highlights done, to brighten up the mousy blonde. They made me look even paler, but at least I was beginning to walk the path walked by women who go to the hairdresser's and the beauty salon to get their nails done.

In class, after Christmas, all the girls had had their first period. Except for me. During recess, they competed to show how bad they felt. Some doubled over, sitting on a bench, because it was cool, it was a "woman" thing.

Boys were afraid and fascinated at the same time.

"Poor Sammy, she is suffering so much, she has her period too."

"My breasts have become huge ... what about you, when did you get your period?"

They broadcast their personal, open secrets amongst the rustling and crunching of crisps, the noise of school bells, gossips and mopeds; they also talked about *that,* like a secret that you don't want to maintain. It was a competition to see who would win the race to grow up.

I kept on moving from one conversation to another, trying to avoid any personal questions, since I hadn't decided whether to tell the truth or not. I was terribly ashamed. I was mad at the world. Even at my parents, whom I considered "genetic" criminals. I had started hating breaks and I often stayed in class, reading magazines on Take That. After the last embarrassing encounter with Tommi, I didn't even want to go out in the common courtyard.

In the first hour we had religion with Father Gomez. He wasn't a Spanish priest, but he enjoyed swearing and had decided to do that in Spanish, in order to sound more exotic and less blasphemous. Moreover, since he resembled Gomez of the Addams Family, he had earned that nickname. Actually, he was from Chioggia, and I'm sure that in Chioggia he swore in the Venetian dialect.

"Holy shit, another day at the office!" It was more of a sacrilegious class than a religion class. Father Gomez was swearing from the moment he stepped into the room, complaining about the government, the Pope and the whores who had become too expensive. We pretended to listen, every now and then we said, "Fuck, you're right. They're assholes!". We would let off unspoken and unauthorised swear words and, in the meantime, we did the homework for the next class, or exchanged notes about the last episode of Gialappa's band, in this mystic atmosphere, all crowded close to the heaters to fight against the bitter cold of the decrepit classrooms in the darkest days of winter.

All of a sudden, the sky darkened. Filippo Lori, who was in 2nd F, opened the door and with a paper megaphone announced the scoop. "That bitch Miss Sferzaferri has just assigned a surprise test. Dante, Boccaccio and a current events essay: *Domenica In and the Chaos Theory.*"

Miss Sferzaferri was our teacher too, so, presumably, we would have to take the same test a couple of hours later. Filippo had asked for permission to go to the bathroom during the test to be a valorous schoolmate and to come and inform us. In other words, he had come to save our bacon.

"Don't shoot the messenger …" he said. Then, before closing the door, he added, "Just thank my big balls!" and showed us the elastic band of his underwear with a snigger.

"Go to Hell!" Father Gomez shouted, sticking to the religious sphere, and chucked him out. Actually, the flames were burning for us now, for the 2nd E. Within a couple of hours, we would have to face the frustration accumulated by Miss Sferzaferri during the Christmas holidays.

She was like Don Quixote, perpetually fighting against imaginary windmills. Every time she arrived in our class, she looked out of breath, she was weighed down by jingling bracelets, had a half-open Hermes bag that vomited scented scarves and a pack of ultra-light Merit cigarettes that she chain-smoked during the lesson. She was like a walking plant dropping leaves. Clumsy, disorganised, spoiled by her own wealth. Super blonde. Super fun. No filters.

"Kids, I have my period today, so don't irritate me," she used to say, before lighting up a cigarette and scattering books and papers all over the desk, like playing bowls. She was chewing bubble gum. Sometimes she cried. It was because of her period, she used to say. I later found out that she was crying because she was divorcing.

My classmates were upset. I kept calm. My grades were high, I wasn't at risk of failing the year. During the last test on Dante, I had written two essays and I had given one to Broncolato, who had received a higher mark than me. Basically, I had exceeded myself.

"Damn, Broncolato, I don't know where you copied it from; but since I can't find the source, I have to give you a very good mark, I have to give you 9!"

Between Religion and the Italian test, we were due to have History of Art. So, we still had an hour to prepare for the test, but the problem was that this time, we didn't have a clue what topics we would be tested on. Miss Sferzaferri used to choose the same essay topics every year. They had never changed in 25 years. Normally, you just needed to photocopy the old tests given to the previous classes and that was it. Easy-peasy.

Della Rosa was the coordinator. He used to get the tests from Miss Spillo. It was a perfect connection to have: the headmaster's 25-year-old secretary, in love with him and willing to give him weekly blowjobs. But apparently not weekly tests!

Vogliatti, instead, had simply fucked the whole school, so she had an ex-boyfriend in every class. One way or another, at least 2 days before a test, we got the topics in the form of notes, wrinkly sheets and word of mouth.

That time though, Miss Sferzaferri had decided to fuck with us. Surprise test with undefined topics, only vaguely reported by a messenger with the brain of a penis. Why did she want to fuck with us? I don't know if it was because of her period, or because she was trying to quit smoking or because of her divorce, but her personal life was about to determine the destiny of 2nd E.

Before facing the Inferno of the quiz, I had to pass through another circle of Hell: one hour of History of Art with Mr Baldassar.

"Innocenti, come here! I want to see if you've grown up."

Mr Baldassar was a giant in every way, physically (he had enormous shoulders) and professionally, since he had been teaching for 35 years. He was a repulsive pervert who only spoke his dialect and would give you marks on the basis of the size of your breasts and of the shape of your butt. The boys could only dream of passing.

"Tell me about Caravaggio," he ordered. As I presented the meagre information I had about the great painter, Mr Baldassar peeked at me from the tip of my shoes to my almost non-existent breasts. With my psychedelic polo neck jumper, for a strange optical illusion, they could have looked bigger than they actually were.

"… considering Cimabue's influence …"

"Enough, Innocenti! It's a 7. Te ghe un bel cul." (Venetian for 'you have a nice bum'.) "Still no tits, but we're going to have a look in a month." As Mr Baldassar was asking questions to Cristina, tension mounted. She had big breasts, so she would usually get a 9.

"Caravaggio mostly used red, brown and gold …"

Suddenly someone opened the door. It was the second time in two hours. It was like a Mexican soap opera. This time, it was the janitor.

"I'm sorry, Mr Baldassar. The headmaster wants to see you in his office."

General satisfaction.

The class had finished 10 minutes early. An unexpected bonus to plan the tactics and to get ready for the test. Cristina got a 10 – thanks to the push-up bra – and Mr Baldassar stormed out of the room all worried. "*Fe silensio, se vedemo giove, fe i bravi che mancan diese minuti* – Be quiet for the next 10 minutes, please. I'll see you on Thursday." (In Venetian).

Probably he could have been reported for paedophilia or sexual harassment. Anyway, as my mother used to say, that kind of "bullshit" didn't exist back then.

As soon as the door was closed, the classroom became a mess. Everybody started cursing.

"Fuck, I haven't studied."

"Dani, tell me that Miss Spillo spilled the beans."

"If I don't get a pass mark, my parents won't take me to the Maldives."

Everybody surrounded Della Rosa to know if there had been updates. Vogliatti apologised for not having kissed enough boys to get the new test. Everybody whispered, talked, yelled in an almost musical sequence, from adagio to allegro.

Then Broncolato climbed on the desk and whistled with two fingers in his mouth, summoning everyone's attention.

"Guys … guys … calm down. I have an idea."

Calming down when Broncolato had an idea was a really terrible idea.

"Now shut up, we only have 8 minutes left …" Broncolato conducted the orchestra like the leader of a labour strike. "Miss Sferzaferri has gone cuckoo, she has her own shit going on. We all know that. When she comes in and gives us the tests, we will all say, together, that she is wrong. We have to pretend to be clueless. Every one of us, you too, nerds!" he said pointing at me.

He went on. "We'll tell her that she had promised that the test would be in the second week of January, because that's what we agreed on. We will convince her that she, herself, has fixed that date. This is the reason why we have agreed with the English teacher – Mr Quantini – to have an English test today. And we can't have 2 tests in one day." It wasn't a terrible idea, actually.

"Hold on! I have the solution!" Della Rosa shouted. All of a sudden, we seemed like an army discussing war strategies. I thought of the scene in Top Gun, when the pilots watch the slides to outline a flight strategy. Cohesiveness was a good thing in classes like ours. We were united till the end, especially in moments of trouble. Della Rosa had a plan. "There's only one thing to do.

We need to lock her out." He shot a line. Broncolato was ready like a gladiator in the arena.

"Lock her out? Are you insane? How would we lock her out?" he interjected. Grudgingly though, he was tickled by that idea. Della Rosa insisted. "Guys, we will lock her out. End of discussion. We'll block the door with a chair, insert a few hair grips in the lock, and start screaming that we are locked in."

I didn't know whether to be scared or amused. Many times, we had voted to leg it to skip a test. Running would have been a classic strategy. But staying wasn't a conventional strategy. The accidental self-imprisonment could have even sounded plausible, especially if Miss Sferzaferri hadn't known that we had been warned by one of her students, the ambassador of the $2^{nd}$ F. There was big clamour in the classroom. After the initial indignation, we started convincing ourselves that Della Rosa's was the best plan.

We needed some authority though. A hint of good faith, which could have persuaded Miss Sferzaferri.

Broncolato said: "Innocenti will back up our version!" Everybody all of a sudden looked at me. "Your mark average is 9, that woman loves you. When she gets angry behind the door, you will have to reassure her."

"Yes, right. You have to stand up for it. She will never suspect you of messing her around." Della Rosa added.

"Exactly! Great idea!"

"Perfect plan!"

"It's the only way!"

My classmates were staring at me. I was standing at the centre of the 'arena'. None of them were waiting for an answer. But suddenly everybody went quiet. They surrounded me, I felt as if I were in a ring of fire. I had no choice, unless I wanted to be beaten up on the third floor, east wing, of the Liceo Scientifico Newton.

I weakly whispered "OK."

There was a roar, the crowd became thunderous, a mix of clapping hands, approving words and mischievous smiles.

"But what should I do, exactly?" I asked. I had just turned into a lazy gladiator.

And this was mainly because I wanted to take off my nerd armour completely. As if I wanted to move down to a lower grade. From super nerd to almost nerd. From academic egoist to comrade-in-arms. There were 2 minutes left and everybody was getting ready. "It's essential for us to be quiet. Miss Sferzaferri can't hear a sound," ordered Broncolato.

Della Rosa blocked the door, using Camilla's desk, Claudia's hair grips and our noble-who-always-wore-a-green-checked-shirt Guglielmo Guidotti Della Francesca's quill pen.

"Pretend that your castle is under siege, Gugliè!" Francesco Crisciotti felt like reassuring our aristocratic friend using Roman common sense.

I was terribly nervous, like when Matilda had forced me to steal a Tower of London keychain in a Camden Town shop during a study trip. After that, I had never broken the law again. I almost had a stroke caused by the sudden increase in blood pressure and felt embarrassed of the uncontrollable sweating of my armpits.

At least at school they didn't have hidden cameras. But I could have still risked a lifetime suspension, the extradition from the nerds' register, the collapse of my scholastic and professional career, the implementation of painful punishments by my parents and, in general, a permanent sense of embarrassment.

There was a positive aspect, though: if Tommaso Orpali heard about this, maybe I could score points with him. Maybe he would have looked at me differently. I would have become Alice the rebel, Alice the storming, Alice the brave.

"She's coming! She's coming!" Della Rosa was glued to the door, trying to hear the teacher's footsteps, since he couldn't see her through the obstructed lock.

I took three deep breaths and summoned my inner strength: "Alice, grow some balls."

5 seconds later, Miss Sferzaferri was energetically trying to open the door.

"What the hell are you doing? Kids? Did you lock yourself in? I'll kill you. You're dead. Open the door immediately!"

Broncolato pushed me in front of the door and with a pat on my back ordered me to speak. I did what I had to.

"Good morning Miss."

"… Innocenti? Is that you?"

She stopped trying to open the door and for a second, she almost sounded concerned about my safety.

"Yes, Miss, it's me. I think we have a problem …"

"Yes, you do!" She lit up a cigarette for the occasion.

I went on with my farce. "After Mr Baldassar went out, the door got stuck and we couldn't open it anymore. It has been defective for days."

"What the fuck are you talking about? Are you kidding me, Innocenti? Are you making fun of me?"

"No, Miss, of course not, I could never do that to you …"

My classmates had to stop themselves from laughing. Della Rosa put a pencil case in his mouth not to burst out.

"If you're lying to protect your classmates, you're in trouble. You'd better come out. You're one of the best students, I would like to remind you that. But I could lower your marks in a second."

Even Broncolato felt sorry for me after this threat. I could see it in his compassionate eyes. At that point, however, I was in the arena with the tiger and I had to fight.

"No, no, I'm not kidding! We're locked in … look, I'm also trying to open the door, but I can't."

And in a flash of diabolic genius, I pretended to force the door. At this point I had earned my classmates' respect forever, they looked at me, amused and scared at the same time, as if I were a beast in a slaughterhouse. I had sacrificed myself for my classmates, and they knew that the teacher would crucify me for that. And that they would be more or less safe.

"I have my period today as well. Damn it!"

Miss Sferzaferri was fidgeting behind the door, smoking her cigarette and biting the nails of the free hand, her golden bracelets crazily clinked like the heels of her shoes.

Then, all of a sudden, silence. Had she bought it? Had she gone to call the Carabinieri? Had she given up and gone back to her office? Or had she simply gone to the toilet to change her tampon?

After 30 seconds of general mutism, the entire class had burst out loudly clapping hands, chanting like in a stadium and laughing.

It was the victory cry of the $2^{nd}$ E. My classmates lifted me up and made me spin in the air as they sang "We are the champions my friends, we are the champions my friends," and I felt like Freddie Mercury at Earl's Court.

Halfway between the $15^{th}$ parallel and the $69^{th}$ meridian, 2 metres above the floor and 80 centimetres from the ceiling, as I was in a free fall over the lino floor, confident that my schoolmates would have grabbed me, the janitor broke down the door with a ladder that he had used as a medieval battering ram.

I fell miserably on the ground, I looked at the door and I saw Miss Sferzaferri's make-up emerging from a cloud of dust, she stood above me like a tiger before it devours its prey.

The last things I can remember are:

» Claudia's hair grips landing on the janitor's buttocks like crazy syringes;

» the Count's quill pen exploding into a octopuses' ink feast;

» Miss Sferzaferri's white sleeves grabbing me by the hair;

» Tommaso Orpali's admiring look as I was being dragged like a sausage along the corridors of the third floor towards the headmaster's office.

"Alice, I am deeply disappointed." These were Headmaster Mariotti's last words about my teenage confusion, before he sentenced me to 12 literary essays, 4 Calvino's books and a 10-day suspension, starting from the first Monday of the following month. Namely, in coincidence with Sanremo Music Festival.

# CHAPTER 9

## The Camera

My parents faced my suspension clinically. Everything seemed to add up: the cause of my delayed menarche and of my mental confusion could be a hormonal dysfunction. They simply couldn't accept that mine had been a teenage prank and made me undergo many blood tests, abdominal ultrasound exams and brain MRIs. Just to find out, in the end, that I was fine.

Apparently.

They looked at me compassionately, like a cancer patient with untraceable metastases. At school, things had gone back to normal in the best way. I had apologised to Miss Sferzaferri, my father had gone to tell the headmaster about my alleged menstrual infirmity and in the meantime, I had earned my classmates' respect. Including Tommaso's. Since seeing me dragged like a sausage along the corridors, he had decided that I was an interesting person. It was the sort of demerit you need to get a merit.

After my rebellious exploit, I decided not to have my hair in braids anymore, highlighted it blonder and began to use purple nail polish. Every time I met Tommaso in the corridors, I would receive a "hi," followed by an admiring smile. The girls around us smiled at me too and looked at me as if I were the queen of the school. I would walk away bowing my head with a flush on my cheeks, trying not to stumble in my flared jeans, which were wiping the corridors of the entire school.

My one-week suspension hadn't been revoked. I would still serve my sentence starting from the following Monday. And my sentence would be a trip to Nice with a potential encounter with the love of my life, a concert in Sanremo and a wedding in Saint Tropez. I would probably never go back to school. Maybe I would fly to England with Gary, and he would award me with an honorific title, like the Beatles, automatically aristocrat and graduate.

This is what I was thinking about on Friday afternoon, going back home from the catechism course, listening to *Sure,* the new single that was to be released in Sanremo. At home, the environment was relaxed. Mamma was making gnocchi in the kitchen and Papá was struggling with the new VHS camera that a Roche sales representative had given him as a present, in exchange for granting a hospital supply.

My father was technologically disabled, a hopeless case. After hours spent reading the instruction manual, he finally managed to find the power button. He had no clue how to start or stop recording, so he did it randomly and inadvertently. The outcome was extraordinary. He had been able to collect abstracted and post-contemporary tapes for all the 1990s: floor close-ups, my mother swearing in voice-over, monologues and disapproving sighs for himself in the attempt to understand whether the camera was on, sudden changes from a frame to another, zoom and sequences that he could have shot during a rollercoaster ride in Wisconsin.

Every cloud has a silver lining, though: as a result of my father's technological failures I used to periodically receive:

»   cameras;

»   mobile phones;

»   fax machines;

»   computers equipped with mouses and mouse pads with images of drugs or chemotherapeutic treatments.

My mother said that I was the only one who could figure out how these things worked. My father hoped that I would train him, but then his intentions would fade away, when he realised that his difficulties were insurmountable. And I would end up with a heap of high-tech devices.

The sales representative's camera would come with me to Nice. A lucky destiny for a VHS.

"Loredana! Say hi!" My father had finally managed to turn the camera on, and now he was pointing it, upside-down, at the kitchen sink, where my mother was making gnocchi.

"Don't you see that I'm making gnocchi?" my mother answered annoyed, throwing one of the gnocchi at the camera. She was wearing black leather leggings, yellow sponge slippers and a tight indigo pullover. That would have been the first and the only video of Mamma. It portrayed the typical environment of my home in those years. It was a metaphor, where gnocchi were the bombs and my mother a tireless soldier.

In the following sequence, after slipping on a rug and slamming into the corner of a door, my father had reached my bedroom, gasping.

"There she is. Our Leonardo da Vinci!" he exclaimed, to highlight the fact that I was working on a technical drawing. Overestimating his daughter had always been natural for him. I looked at him and replied with a cheerful hi. Smiling at my papá had always been natural for me too.

And that was the very same camera that on the following Monday morning I was pointing outside the window on the Intercity train from Padua to Nice, trying to record the last images of my homeland, knowing that I would probably never come back. The train roared through the hilly countryside near Vicenza, the noxious smell emanating from the factories in the Po Valley, the fog of Verona hills, the jagged coastline from Varazze to Imperia, in Liguria. Laura and I were chilling out in coach 9, compartment 22, listening to Take That repeatedly on our Walkmans. For the occasion we had bought a number of magazines with articles about Take That, crisps promoted by Jason Orange, Coke cans with a Take That theme contest and salami sandwiches, which were Mark Owen's favourites. Moreover, we had a notepad to write down our thoughts and two teddy bears to be thrown at Robbie and Gary on the stage, with love notes and our telephone numbers.

The idea that Gary could dial my home number for real and that my mother could answer the phone terrified me.

"Hi, it's Gary."

She would have mistaken him for a gym equipment salesman. "Who are you? We don't need anything. I only buy Technogym and I only speak French."

"I am Gary, I want to marry Alice."

"Armando! We have a fool on the phone here, would you tell him to fuck off?" Then, she would have hung up. The only man my mother would have made an effort to learn English for was Don Johnson, the central character of Miami Vice, my mother's secret dream. The man she used to spend 3 hours a day with, every afternoon from 2 to 5 p.m., when she watched the show on Channel 4. If my dream was to marry Gary Barlow, hers was to move to Miami with Don and chase the Mexican Mob aboard offshore boats.

From the bottom of my heart, I hoped that Gary would call at the right time, when I would answer the phone. And that my mother would really move to Miami to sell exercise bikes.

It was freezing on the train. It was impossible to look sexy in that cold. Believe me, I tried hard. It was so cold that I had to put on the woollen jumper that Nonna Tilda had made for me, my father's ski jacket and the thick hat from my ice-skating days. My skinny jeans and my semi-transparent, ethnic-patterned t-shirt had disappeared under all those clothes.

Even so, I would have undressed immediately for Gary. I would have practised my undressing techniques for the entire trip to Nice, with Laura timing me. Then we would chew bubble gum, sing all the songs of the last album, *Nobody Else*, comment on the photo stories on *Cioè* magazine and, most importantly, we would dream, dream a lot.

After all, there were still 6 hours to go before arriving in Nice.

# CHAPTER 10

## Montecarlo

"Run! Run!"

I was gasping, screaming and running in the woods at the same time, chased by 2 French-speaking pit bulls.

"I can't see anything. Which way should we go?"

Panic. Laura had lost track of me and had stopped in the icy bushes to try to find me in the obsidian night.

"Come on! You need to climb the fence!"

I stretched my arm from the top of the fence, and she grabbed it to save herself. We could hear the dogs barking and the policemen growling in the distance. We could see the flashlights in the thorny garden of the Grand Hotel de la France.

We made it. Once on the top of the fence, we jumped down onto the street, into the unrestricted real world from where we had come. Once again, a tall and sharp fence separated us from the men of our dreams. That night we learned that, in life, any fences could be climbed over.

"Don't tell me that you've recorded this. Have you recorded it?"

"What does it mean if the light is red?"

"It means that it's still recording! Give me that thing, you moron!"

In the previous hours, incredible events and surprising co-incidences had led us to the fence of Grand Hotel de la France, with our clothes half-ripped, our hearts in our throats and our hands covered with mud.

Once at the station in Nice, we had called our local contacts and we had immediately gone to the airport, where both Take That and their archenemies – the Enemies – were expected to land later in the afternoon. We didn't know the exact time of

69

their arrival, so we were ready to wait for 8 hours if we had to. At the airport, we had arranged to meet Valentina, a groupie from Genoa. She was a real celebrity, since she was in the video of *Could It Be Magic* and, more importantly, she had been interviewed by *Cioè* Magazine. There was a rumour that she had slept with all the members of the band, and she was just 16. We didn't know whether to hate her or to admire her, so in doubt we had decided to worship her.

We were meeting Samantha and Deborah too, both with an "h" in the name. It goes without saying that musical fanaticism was overrepresented by lower class girls who had Italian names but with an 'h', or inspired by Hollywood stars, and so I was mostly surrounded by names with an "h" or inspired by Hollywood stars. I was attracted by these friendships. I liked spending my time with girls who said "fuck," who had long black nails and worked at their mothers' hair salons on Saturdays. I was fascinated by such a grown, real and free world, by that spirit according to which you could do whatever you wanted in life, because things could only get better for you. In that world, if you moved to London to work as a shop assistant in a perfume shop you would become a celebrity in your hometown. I wanted to be exactly like them. Genuine, free, saying "fuck", chewing bubble-gum with my mouth open and wearing pink lip gloss.

I always kept my middle-class origins hidden. I was ashamed of that and, above all, I wanted to seem "cool". I didn't want to justify myself.

"Aren't you too smart to be a groupie?"

"Aren't you too posh to be a fan?"

They would have never told me, but they would have thought it straight away, so I preferred to seem humble and proletarian and to imagine myself working as a shop assistant in Brianza.

I had seen Samantha and Deborah – who were from Naples – in a picture, and I had sent them a photograph of myself after we had exchanged messages through *Cioè* magazine. We were like arranged married couples who know each other by correspondence.

They were chattering about piercings and tattoos. Deborah had a tattoo on her wrist. It was a T for Take That. Samantha had had her tongue pierced because she wanted the same ring as Howard's.

"Did it hurt?" I pretended to be interested, or maybe I didn't pretend at all. "When I'm 18 I'll get my navel pierced. I know that there are these piercings with a small chain where you can put your name. I would like to put Gary." I pretended I wanted to get pierced, or maybe I didn't pretend at all. When I turned 18 I actually did it.

Three hours had gone past, and we had made friends with all the 'important authorities,' which in our jargon were all the people who could give us truthful and useful information about Take That. Tip-offs, previews, news. At the airport, the important authorities were cleaners, security guards, hostesses, porters, taxi drivers, shop assistants and whoever had a badge with a picture on it.

We asked everybody if they knew the airline, the time of arrival or the hotel where Take That would stay. We moved in small groups. It was a kind of a competition. Every group of fans could be made up of no more than 5 people, because only one girl could marry each band member.

Every group was against the other. You couldn't share the information you had, otherwise too many fans would have known where the hotel was, too many fans would have been too close to them. Too many fans might scupper our chances.

Most people replied, "I don't know". Others smiled, maybe remembering when they were young. Some fooled us and made up names, places and dates. But a few of them, those who really knew something, sometimes helped us, maybe because they had teenage daughters too and understood the situation. Or maybe because we bribed them with 20,000 lire.

We were still chilling out on the floor, after almost 4 hours waiting in front of the international arrivals, when we suddenly heard some girls screaming. Maybe it was a false alarm, like the previous 23. Every time a plane landed, we all stood up excited and crowded at the exit, just to find out that the airport had spewed out only North African passengers, skateboarders from Tennessee and Pakistani women wrapped up in red silk drapes.

This time the screaming was louder. Valentina – the groupie from Genoa with platinum blonde hair, a doll's face and full lips – threaded her way through the crowd.

It wasn't Take That.

Unbelievable.

It was the Enemies, as we called them. They were greeted with a mix of "Boo!", "Wow!", "Go away!", "Come here!", "I hate you" and "I love you." Overall, though, there was a widespread excitement for having seen someone famous in person.

Personally, I found them even uglier than they looked on TV, but it was a key moment of our adventure, so I turned my camera on, and I was recording everything. Then I got distracted. Valentina had started talking to one of the band's guys she had already slept with in the past, to console herself for not marrying Mark. In a few seconds she disappeared with the musicians.

"Whore! Slut!" the crowd screamed. We all followed them to the car park outside the airport. A river of fans eager to witness Valentina's destiny. I was very nervous. I was afraid to see something I wasn't ready for. Valentina was escorted to a black, tinted-window van that was parked out there. One by one, all the members of the band followed her inside the car.

"Maybe she's just getting their autographs." None of us wanted to think about what was really happening there. We were little girls with posters on our bedrooms' walls, schoolgirls who wrote "I love you" on their diaries, children who still needed their mothers to buy some new pants. We were not emotionally ready.

After 15 endless minutes, Valentina was pushed outside the van. The door closed and the vehicle left speeding away. Her face was a mask, with hair and make-up messed up. The mascara had trickled down her cheekbones and the lipstick was all around her mouth. She had an absent, almost ethereal look as she fixed up her black bustier's shoulder straps and the zip of her jeans. At that moment, I felt really sorry for her. Whoever had let that 16-year-old girl dye her hair like that, dress like that and get her nose pierced, had given her permission to get in that van as well.

Maybe she had a dysfunctional family. Maybe her mother was an alcoholic and her father had abandoned them. Maybe she worked at her grandmother's sewing shop to eke out a living or was forced to sell her body to her brother's friends to avoid being beaten. Maybe the boybands were her only shelter.

But the fans were pitiless: "You whore!"

"You'd like that, wouldn't you?" Valentina replied proudly. Then she walked away, swaying her hips, headed to a cab. I never saw her again, except on the magazines.

"Did you record this? Don't tell me you did!" asked Laura. I noticed the red light on the camera.

"I didn't do that on purpose. I forgot to turn it off." A part of me was unintentionally still on too. I couldn't stop asking myself what had happened in that van. What would happen when you grew up? Wouldn't you have the chance to say no anymore? Would you have to kiss a man and say 'yes' all the time? Would you have to let men have sex with you without questioning? Like a kind of initiation, to prove yourself worthy to join the adult world?

If those were the conditions, I thought, I would rather play with the Smurfs for the rest of my life. I wasn't ready to be violated. How could you raise invisible barriers when you were a woman? Maybe you could buy those private property defences they have in America. I had seen on a documentary. You could place them all around your garden and they were invisible. If someone tried to cross them, though, he would get electrified. Could you grow up without having sex, or did you have to become a sliding door for all those who wanted to come in and out? Maybe that was what experience meant. Getting stronger. Suffering. Making sacrifices. Maybe you just needed to protect your heart and let the body fight.

Maybe Valentina had been sent to fight early, while I still lived in my castle of affection and innocence, in my room of posters and diamond-patterned wallpaper, among my Smurfs and my Barbie collections, among the homemade gnocchi and Miss Sferzaferri's quizzes. Maybe Alice wasn't ready to leave her Wonderland.

I was upset. After the shock of witnessing a publicly enabled violation. I almost didn't feel like seeing Gary anymore. I had never got so close to sex and I was terrified. In my mind Take That were nearly transcendental figures, only capable of writing love poems and sending marriage proposals. Still, maybe they were human too, just like the Enemies, capable of locking you in a black van.

As those thoughts crossed my mind, together with the vision of my father shaking his head in dismay, a security agent came close to us and whispered to follow him, without attracting attention, which meant we had to restrain our joy from showing up on our faces, fake indifference toward the potentially best day of our lives and maintain secrecy about information of 'national' interest; making us the most visible people in the whole airport.

Our informer was a white man in his fifties who had been moved after he had looked at Deborah's big breasts 30 minutes earlier.

"It's useless for you to wait here. The plane has already landed. They will go and pick them up on the runway with a blue Mercedes van. They will leave the airport from the cargo exit in 4 minutes. Now, if someone asks, I haven't told you anything."

After one last glance at Deborah's tits and, this time, at my legs as well, he went back to where he had come from: a magic place beyond the metal detectors.

4 minutes.

Cargo exit.

The two pieces didn't match.

Especially because we couldn't run.

If we had run, everybody would have understood what was going on and would have run with us.

To get there on time, however, we had to walk fast.

Panic.

Adrenaline.

"Fuck!" was Deborah's first reaction.

Our hearts in our throats, where we had left them.

"Where the fuck is the cargo exit?" asked Laura.

We were all thinking the same thing.

The other words were "How fucking long does it take to get to the cargo exit?" and also "How do we get to the fucking cargo exit?"

Luckily, we were a strong team, so we managed to coordinate quietly. Deborah found out where the cargo exit was, Samantha suggested to take a cab, I comforted the group by saying "Calm down, girls. We still have 120 seconds."

What followed was a sequence worthy of a post-modern film editing experiment.

We rushed into a cab, begged the taxi driver to take us quickly to the cargo exit, which was only 150 metres away, while the blue van was driving past us. In that moment, as I handed 50,000 lire to the taxi driver, I had the chance to speak the words that only a restricted selection of human beings can pronounce during their miserable lifetime.

"Follow that car!"

"You mean the van?"

And there we were: Laura, Deborah, Samantha and myself, crowded in a yellow cab with beaded seat mats, our heads outside the windows and our arms stretched towards the blue van speeding around the hairpin turns of Monte Carlo, chased by a taxi driver from Marseille who thought he was Michael Schumacher.

My camera recorded our screams, our swearing and the incredulous excitement. My camera recorded the blue van's windows going down and Mark Owen waving 'Hello'. My camera recorded my shrill voice when Gary sent me a kiss from the rear window.

"I'm gonna die! I'm gonna die! I'm gonna die!"

If someone had listened to that recording without watching the footage, they would have thought that it dealt with a bombing or with mothers whose children had just been hit by a car. In that fifteen-minute of apocalyptic chase there was agony, there was adrenaline.

The red light on my camera was still flashing as the gates of the Hotel de la France opened like the gates of Heaven, and our cab followed, undisturbed, the blue van inside the residence of Take That.

"Good luck!" sneered our driver from Marseille, "I bet that you won't even get to the lift," he predicted before skidding away.

However, with our ripped backpacks, our chewing gum and our hands full of marker-drawn hearts, not only we believed that we would have got to the lifts, but also that we would have got into their rooms. We were so close!

But we were fooling ourselves. Our "backpackers' look" could not be disguised in a five-star hotel in Monte Carlo, where the stars were worth double.

We just needed the lift doors to open and we could have pushed any button to run from the staff at the front desk.

"Where are you going, ladies?" shouted the front desk manager who had noticed the intruders. We could have told the truth, but we didn't know what the truth was. *Where were we actually going? What was our destination? A new life? Love? Destiny? A bedroom scattered with rose petals? A place without inhibitions and virginity?*

Maybe we should just have said "We would just like to take the lift". But we didn't say a word. We just looked at each other and took the fire exit behind us, running through the bushes in the night, as if we had stolen something.

That's how we had ended up running away from the French police and from the two big pit bulls in the dark garden of the Hotel de La France.

We were intruders in a private property without a reservation. Maybe we were burglars. We had stolen a dream, an illusion of happiness. When the adults had seen us, we had reminded them of when they were young themselves, and now they were chasing us to take back what they had lost.

During the escape, we had lost something too. We had lost two of us. "Hopefully they haven't been caught. We have the Festival tomorrow."

With that sweet thought in our minds, Laura and I set out for the hairpin turns of Montecarlo, after a long day spent being our own stunt men, looking for the famous hotel my mother had booked for us. The same hotel where Liz Taylor had stayed.

# CHAPTER 11

## Sanremo

The hotel where Liz Taylor had stayed must have changed management. I was sure that Liz Taylor hadn't slept in a bedroom covered in red velvet, with no windows and a mirror right above the canopy bed.

Who knows what number my mother had called?

We didn't pay much because we had reached the place late, and it was a pay by the hour hotel. The owner was a fat Croatian woman. She had a blonde buzz cut and purple lipstick that had stained her teeth.

We told her our story and she wished us good luck. "Come back here with Take That when you marry them!" The woman said goodbye with a thunderous laugh. She had more important clients waiting at the desk. Before we left, she added: "We also organize wedding banquets here!"

For a moment, I pictured myself wearing a synthetic fabric wedding dress, red leg warmers and my hair crimped, in the middle of a Las Vegas style flash wedding, among tables full of crisps and cold appetizers.

"Thank you. We will think about it!" replied Laura, dragging me out.

After an hour on a train along the French coastline and 10 minutes in a taxi, we finally reached the legendary Ariston Theatre in Sanremo. We were exhausted, dirty and badly dressed. But we imagined that, in the best case scenario, they would have filmed us from the waist up, hidden behind our signs "Gary I love you" "Robbie marry me" and "Jason you are my life", so nobody would have noticed our 'urban-gypsy' appearance.

After all, we were not simply individuals, we represented a specific category: The Fans. Nobody would have judged our cleanliness or our beauty, but only the level of our madness and carefree, deluded youth. The camera operators would have focused on those who screamed louder, cried more desperately and on those who threw their bras on the stage. For the occasion I had stolen Matilda's black lace bra and put it in the pocket of my jeans. And at the same time, I had forgotten to wear one, which would have been useless anyway, leaving my timid breasts uncovered under my white corduroy top. Maybe I could have been included in the category 'Girls in jeans and a white shirt who look good even without their make-up on,' but at the time I didn't think I was cute enough.

Laura was wearing a shocking pink top, which showed her navel and her flat belly. Her sharp, fake nails were shocking pink too. She had applied them 10 minutes earlier by using some glue she had bought at a department store called Upim. Every time she raised the sign to practise for the show, a nail would come off, and Laura would spend half an hour kneeling down on the floor, looking for it amongst strangers' shoes.

We reached our seats, which were not in the real front row, as we thought, but in the 'audience' front row, which meant the first row behind the three VIP rows. Technically, we were in the fourth row, on the left side of the stage. We were close enough to be seen and heard, close enough to make objects land on the stage like vows to gods: plush toys, bras and love notes. There was a risk, as well, that it would all fall on the heads of the old bags in the front row or get stuck in the backcombed hair of some director's mother-in-law.

"Do you think they remember us?"

*Of course, they do. After all, they saw us yesterday for 12 seconds from a van speeding at 100 kilometres per hour.*

"Maybe they will invite us to the hotel tonight."

*Sure. They could throw notes at us from the stage, dedicate a song to us or speak to us with a mic. Of course, they will invite us. No doubt about it.*

The audience was made of:

» 5% VIP;

» 10% ordinary people;

» 85% fans.

We were insignificant tiny dots of a straight line that Take That would have never noticed. In that case, we had plan B. We would sneak off to the lobby where we had an appointment with the cousin of the janitor who worked in the building where Laura's aunt lived. He was a florist. He would give us two uniforms and we would change very quickly in the bathroom while the unaware audience would applaud Bocelli or some other music minority. Then we would get two cheap bunches of daisies and step into the changing rooms, pretending to be delivering flowers. The appointment was at 9:29 p.m., 5 minutes after the band's last song.

Our plan was perfect. We had no idea where the changing rooms were or how many bodyguards we would find at the door, but it was the 1990s and bouncers in the 1990s were harmless. Most of them used fake earpieces, just to pretend they were connected to someone. They were like those toy guns you could remove the red tip from. My mother had one of them in a drawer.

"It keeps dopers away, but not professional burglars," she used to say.

And we were professional groupies. We could distinguish a fake earpiece from a real one. We just had to wait now. In the meantime, the show had started. We were wrapped up in the red velvet of the theatre, stunned by the spotlights, the screams and the clapping of fanatical fans. There was adrenaline in the air.

Pippo Baudo, the host, was entertaining the audience with gags here and there before the live coverage was going to start. "We have a heap of dreams here tonight. Can you feel it?"

He was talking about the dreams of a thousand girls who were in love, the dreams of unknown young singers, the dreams of all the people watching from home, who, for one night at least, would not worry about the mortgage or their drug-addicted son.

In those years, you could not take pictures to share or tag. The only thing you could do was dream, keeping a hand on your heart to slow it down.

Performance after performance, we were getting closer to the crucial moment. We kept staring at Pippo Baudo, who ran around the stage like a reed in a dinner suit being moved by the wind. I kind of loved him. He was so paternal. Every now and then, he talked to the groupies who had filled the theatre.

"Come on, girls. You just have to wait for a few more minutes!" Applause, tears, bras. Rai 1's audience share must have had reached unbelievable peaks.

It was 9:22 p.m. when Pippo Baudo turned around and looked our way. One minute of silence. It seemed like he had forgotten the words, but it was an intentional silence; "Guess who's next?"

Our hands began to shake. Laura and I hugged each other and started jumping and crying, crushing feet, shoes and Laura's nails which were lost on the floor.

Then we blacked out. Like plane crash survivors. We stopped being aware of what was happening. We couldn't grasp anything. Take That were finally on the stage. It was a shock.

The song was *Sure*. Gary was singing and the others were breakdancing.

"Gaaaaaary!" I screamed so loudly that my vocal cords could have exploded. I raised my arms, waving the sign. Teddy bears and chocolates were being thrown on the stage from everywhere.

He was my love. So close, and yet so far. This was my chance. When would I be able to stand so close to him again? "Gaaaaaary!" But my shout sank among those of thousands of other girls, who were in love just like me.

I couldn't get his attention. The only thing I succeeded in was bursting the eardrums of the old ladies sitting in the front row. We got everything wrong. Laura and I were screaming two different names at the same time, to start with. Our voices were cancelling each other out. We were insignificant. Two voices in the ocean of voices.

It was as if the Teletext had thrown up all of its messages in the form of human beings, who were now throwing up those same messages on the stage of Sanremo.

In the end we hugged each other and began to cry. It was the funeral of a possibility; the temporary ending of something we had been thinking about for the last 3 months. We had failed.

We still had the plan B, though. As Take That were collecting all the objects which had landed on the stage, Laura and I were ready to sneak out and to put on our florist disguises.

That night, my father had tuned in to Italia 1, the wrong channel. I had told him Rai 1, but he had misunderstood. Then he got carried away watching 'Dead Poets Society' and missed the deadly poetic moment when his daughter had been filmed as she was throwing her black lace bra.

Broncolato, on the contrary, had recorded everything, including my moment of glory. I was eternally grateful to him; even though I would later have to return the favour by writing an essay on Boccaccio or by doing a technical drawing for him at school.

"Move! Run!"

Laura was dragging me to the exit door. Outside, the Theatre was completely empty, except for journalists and paparazzi positioned at the entrance. For a moment they had turned their flashes on, thinking that we were two singers, but then they had realised that we were just two dorky girls with signs in their hands and flared jeans, and they had put down their cameras.

"He said to the right side, lateral car park," Laura said.

"Do you think that's him? The guy with the Beetle car saying 'Flowers'?

Choosing a Beetle to sell flowers did have some kind of botanical consistency.

"Ennio!"

Laura ran in the night towards the next adventure.

"Hey girls! So, have you seen them?"

His question sounded rhetorical to me, but then I looked at him in the face and realised that I had overrated him. He had probably never been awarded with a Nobel Prize for Cleverness.

"Of course, we have! We were in the Theatre! Everybody's seen them!" Laura answered laughing. "They haven't heard us, though. It was a bloody mess in there!"

Bloody. Another "adult" word, together with "fuck".

Ennio was in his thirties and he clearly owed something to Laura's mother, who was from Genoa, like him.

"Put these uniforms on quickly and go in through the artists' entrance."

"Thank you!"

"You're welcome. If you succeed, that will be great publicity for my shop. But it's hard. They have never let me in."

Two minutes later, we were officially working for Ennio's Flowers Ltd., wearing our blue prison uniform with the logo of the company on our chest.

We had changed inside the van to save time, and now we were walking towards the artists' exit, bearing small bunches of pink daisies and 2 notes for 'Gari' and 'Robi', the Italian version of their real names, reinterpreted by Ennio, the florist.

"You speak to the bouncer," ordered Laura. After she heard what had happened with Miss Sferzaferri, I was considered an expert in the field.

"What should I tell him?" I was nervous.

"Tell him that we need to deliver these flowers but that we don't know who they are for, so he won't think that we are groupies."

The idea of mispronouncing the names of the band members was brilliant. Every fan would have pronounced them perfectly, with a Manchester accent, revealing their real identity.

Therefore, as we walked to the door, in my mind I had started practising the wrong pronunciation in order to be ready. Tac Dat, Gheby and Robert. Tik Tak. Cary and Lobby …

As soon as we reached the exit a huge Norwegian bouncer, who looked like Hulk Hogan, stopped us at the door straight away.

"What are those?" he asked, looking at the flowers. Maybe he had been instructed to always ask the same question. Maybe he was blind. Or maybe he was an idiot.

"Flowers. We need to deliver them."

"To who?"

Apparently, the idiot had other questions to ask.

"We don't know. The names are here … they must be those British singers."

I started reading the names out loud, crippling the pronunciation.

The big idiot took the bait. He didn't understand that we were just two fans.

"OK. In you go!"

He opened the door. We were blinded by a godly light, and a wedding soundtrack filled our imagination. The die was cast.

We would meet our husbands-to-be at the end of the corridor and maybe we would change the bouquet. Daisies were way too cheap.

It was a moment when it was fundamental to keep quiet and to focus on the following rules:

» do not look each other in the eyes;

» do not stumble;

» do not smile;

» do not tell jokes;

» do not look upwards.

In short, we behaved like two Mafia hit men. We just had to go straight on, walk down the corridor, avoid agents, artists and sound technicians and find the changing room. After all, we were two florists from Genoa, and we were behaving accordingly. Time seemed suspended.

"Hey, you! Where are you going?"

An official-looking little bitch with red glasses stopped us after a few steps.

"We need to deliver these flowers."

"Well, you can give them to me, I'll take care of it. You can go out now."

In less than no time, she snatched our dreams from us, by snatching the daisies out of our hands.

We went back with our tails between our legs and the faces of inconsolable children who had just dropped their ice-cream on the floor.

"You haven't missed anything."

The bitchy secretary was talking to us.

Before we stepped out the door, she smiled at us sadistically and said: "They've already left for London. Secret exit."

Outside, Ennio was waiting for us with trepidation. Apparently, we had not disappointed him. The simple fact that his logo had entered the building through the 'artists' entrance was a great thing. He gave us 2 bunches of roses to thank us. He was smoking a cigarette in front of the entrance of the Theatre while we were telling him about our adolescence, with our uniforms still on.

I was sorrowful. Another failure.

The adrenaline for the adventure was fading away. We had nothing left to do but to go back to Padua with great sadness in our hearts. The only consolation was that we could lie and depict a different reality.

I had the video from Montecarlo. I had appeared on Rai 1. I could always have made up an interesting story. Above all, I was relieved by the fact that no one would ever see me dressed like a florist!

"Alice! What are you doing here?"

Suddenly a hand touched my shoulder.

# CHAPTER 12

## The Sprinklers

What was Tommaso Orpali doing in Sanremo?

I wanted to disappear.

Not only it was obvious that I was a Take That fan – which already by itself could be interpreted as a sign of immaturity – but also that I was also dressed like a florist. Laura understood the significance of this serendipitous encounter and bolted towards Ennio.

"What are you doing here?" I asked, almost begging.

"Mamma, come here. I want you to meet a schoolmate of mine!" Tommaso turned around and called an elegant, back-combed-haired woman in her fifties. Maybe my bra had landed on her head earlier.

"Hello. So you work in Sanremo!" she said after scrutinising me from head to toe.

"Good evening, madam. Well, I'm actually dressed like this because I was trying to sneak into the dressing rooms." My mouth took over.

"Marvellous! I attempted to do the same when I was in Venice, at the Lido. I wanted to meet Tyrone Power!"

Turning on her heels, her Hermes handbag fluttering in the air, Mrs Orpali went back to her car.

"What are you up to tonight?"

I couldn't believe that. He was asking me, only me, what I was up to that night, apart from delivering flowers.

"My mother wanted to see Bocelli, you know, and she wanted me to go with her. I have kind of had enough now." He talked as if he needed a justification too.

I had about 3 seconds to figure out the best answer. If I had said "no", that I was not available, that I had to deliver more flowers or that I had to go back to the hotel with Laura, I might have triggered his interest, because he might have felt refused. Tommaso might have dreamed about the moment I would finally say "yes." He might have wallowed in the thought of meeting me again at school. Maybe he might have even touched himself in the shower thinking of me naked at a Take That concert.

"No" was surely the best option.

"Yes. I'm free tonight." My mouth was still in charge.

"Would you like to go for a walk?"

*A walk? Why don't we have an ice cream too? Why don't we walk as we eat our ice creams, so we go straight back into the 1950s?*

"OK. *Sounds great.*" I replied in English. My English would show up in the most embarrassing moments, just to make an awkward situation even more awkward.

"Laura! Tommaso has just asked me out!"

I ran to tell her the great news and words followed me like the Doppler Effect.

"Fuck, fuck, fuck!"

Laura had drawn words from her most erudite dictionary to express her unforeseen delight.

Judging from the quantity of "fucks" she had pronounced since the beginning of our journey, she was at least 2 years older than she was when we had left home.

"What are you going to do? Do you want to bang him? Have you brushed your teeth?"

"You sound like my mother! Of course I have brushed my teeth! Lucky I've spent the last 30 minutes surrounded by flowers, so I don't stink. And we are not doing anything anyway. We'll just go for a walk."

"Oh my God! I told you that this was going to be the night! I thought you would fuck Gary, but Tommaso Orpali is not a bad alternative!"

"Come on, stop it. You're making me anxious. It's just a walk. You need to get Ennio to take you back to the hotel."

Before we could change our minds, Tommaso and I were walking down the Sanremo seafront. Or better, Tommaso was walking down the seafront with a Ligurian florist. My heart was pounding.

Tommaso was a fling. Gary was still the love of my life.

To be honest, Tommaso was much taller than Gary. He was sexy, too. At least as sexy as Gary. To be honest, he was more charming than the Swiss Milker. To be honest, I probably liked him as much as I liked the Mancunian singer, but with the corporeal advantage. To be honest, I wasn't being honest. I liked Tommaso even more than I liked Gary, and he was real, and that scared me to death.

We walked down Via Volturno to Piazza Sardi, where Tommaso had been told the only ice-cream shop still open was.

And then I realised that Tommaso was as shy as I was.

As he was walking, he kept looking down, he was short of breath and it was as if he was searching for the right words to break the silence and the freezing cold of the Ligurian winter. He threw them out, like fire tipped arrows that heated up the air for a while, but died out rapidly. As he was talking, I imagined a medieval archer shooting towards a dark forest. Some words would have gone out in the darkness, some could have set fire to the trees, but in the end, no arrow could have lit up the whole night.

He was like a burning sun. He was shining. The sun was in his eyes, in his movements, in his emotions. The sun was in his inability to manage the situation. There is always a bright halo around naïve people.

"So … when are you going back to Padua? You're a tough girl, by the way. I've heard that you have been suspended for locking Miss Sferzaferri out of the classroom. Respect." He said.

"Oh, well … yes, I have been suspended. But I must admit that it wasn't my idea, so I don't deserve respect." I smiled.

My florist's uniform automatically made me a badass, as if being a florist had made me 5 years older within 5 minutes. I felt like a proletarian girl. I felt more expert, someone with real tits and and a real job.

"I've been readmitted, anyway … luckily I have a very high average grade, otherwise I would have failed the year for sure!" I explained.

As long as we stuck to simple conversation, my arrow-words were long-range, but we were getting closer to the scary, dark forest. When we got to the ice-cream shop, we decided that buying an ice cream was a good idea, even though it was January. After all, when two people have the same bad idea at the same time, the idea turns into a great idea.

"Hazelnut and chocolate. Whipped cream on top, please." I requested. It was a classic, like pizza. I always had margherita.

"Custard and pistachio," for Tommaso. I had always been suspicious of people who ordered fruit-flavoured ice creams. Ice creams must be made of cream. I thought that people who ordered mango and lemon ice creams should have been admitted to a rehab clinic to regain their love for life.

My repulsion originated from a childhood trauma. When I was a little girl and I did not behave myself at a restaurant, my mother would order a fruit salad to punish me. Since then, I had always associated fruit with punishment, a downgraded version of any culinary experience.

Tommaso had passed the ice cream test. Fortunately, he was one of those people that I considered normal.

While we were walking, he looked at me and laughed.

"You're like a 5-year-old child! You have something all over your face and you haven't even realised."

"No … what's on my face?"

"A lot of cream! Come here …"

Since before I was born – even in utero – I had always excelled in my inability to coordinate my arms to complete a meal without getting dirty, even on the most unimaginable parts of my body.

If I ate rigatoni with pesto, at the end of the meal, I would have basil and pine nuts all over my back. Or, when I bit a slice of pandoro, I would end up puffing powdered sugar all around the living room. I was a sort of obsessive-compulsive stainer.

During my first 15 years of life I had actively contributed to the income of the laundry detergent companies.

Since my face was covered in cream, Tommaso felt the need to wipe it with his mother's floral handkerchief, which he had suddenly pulled out of his pocket. He started to gently remove the cream from my lips.

"I don't feel comfortable with this, sorry."

I drew back, unwittingly.

He drew back, unwittingly.

The ice cream had not turned out to be such a great idea. I had an out of body experience; like when I was watching TV with my parents and an embarrassing scene threatened to get even more awkward and I dreamed of escaping the room.

"So, why do you like the *fat one*?"

After the clumsy attempt to clean my face, Tommaso had begun to talk about Take That, switching to "subjects she may be interested in".

"First of all, his name is Gary and he is not fat. He is just well built. And he is the brains of the band."

"Hahaha! The brains? Sorry, but it's hard to believe that there is a brain there."

"Believe what you want, it's easy to judge when you don't know. I bet that you don't even have any of their CDs."

"Luckily not. I listen to Pearl Jam. I don't like pop music. But judging from the quantity of fans they have, Take That must have some kind of talent. I must admit it. It's just that you seem too smart to slobber over 5 tacky dancers. Is there anyone you like? I mean … anyone real?"

*Real.* Tommaso was surely real, and his question was even more real. But I didn't have a real or a really meaningful answer.

"For now, I only like people on posters and video tapes."

"Video tapes?"

"Yes. My father has a camera."

"Really? Is he a director? I thought he was a doctor."

"Yes, he is a doctor. That's why they shouldn't give him cameras. Cancer can't be filmed, so he always ends up filming my mother making gnocchi, or me drawing rhombuses or hexagonal projections for my technical drawing class."

"Hahaha! You're funny, as well as cute."

*Cute.* If your best friend or your classmate who only wanted you to help him with Latin translations said this, that would be a compliment. But when the man you daydream about says you're cute? It sounds a bit like an insult. Why not "beautiful"? Maybe "cute" is what you say to a little girl who is not a woman yet.

Still, he made me blush and, for a moment, I didn't say a word.

"So, tell me, what kind of videos are we talking about?"

"Car chases, concerts, swear words. I've done almost nothing. The camera started recording by itself and I forgot to turn it off."

"I'd love to watch them. Do you know I do editing too? I edit images and add music, instead of doing my homework."

"I'd rather die! You already think that I am a dorky little girl, if I showed you the videos of Take That, I would have no chance left."

"Chance of what?"

There I was. Alice playing Alice. Vomiting words because of my verbal diarrhea. It was like sky diving: I had no chance of getting back on board. Right then I hoped this incontinence was more like bungee jumping, with words that would eventually bounce back on their elastic cords.

Tommaso looked amused, as if he knew what I meant but wanted to hear it from me. We stood facing each other under a weeping willow (I never knew whether it was a weeping willow or some other tree, and I never learnt how to distinguish one plant from another, but, poetically speaking, I liked to think that it was a weeping willow and not just a common maritime pine).

I stood there, in my florist uniform, with whipped cream around my lips. He stood there, with his short-sleeved army jacket and his long and cold fingers. I stood there, with my strained, toothy smile, like a celebrity in a wax museum. He stood there, with his glasses fogging up in the cold air and his eager eyes.

We stood there like two idiots, about to kiss each other.

All of a sudden, I began to notice all the extremities of my body. My oblong big toe against the tip of my Converse shoes. My fingernails eaten up by stress. My hair knotted by too many fanatical leaps and cold sweat at the concert. My breasts, barely visible and lacking any sexual authority.

Another out of body experience. In the meantime, I was reviewing the tips I had read on French kisses in my mind, trying to remember whether the tongue had to rotate clockwise or anticlockwise.

Was it supposed to happen this way? In a park, in Sanremo, on a cold January night?

Tommaso had stopped smiling and activated his "I am serious, now I'm going to kiss you" expression.

He slowly took my hands in his hands, crossing his fingers with mine, then he gently raised them and pulled me closer to him.

*Alice, the bad news is that you will not kiss Gary Barlow. The good news is that you will finally kiss someone.* My heart was pounding like the boiler in my 1960s apartment when my mother took a shower after being on the exercise bike. My unripe breasts stung like pins on my pullover. I felt an unfamiliar fire between my legs and a sense of all over tingling and imminent faint. Perhaps I was diabetic like my father.

Tommaso let go of my right hand to caress my chin. He gently raised my head and came even closer. It was time to close my eyes and think of Brooke and Ridge snogging like there was no tomorrow in The Bold and the Beautiful, episode 11.

And then …

Rain.

We were hit by a cold gush of unexpected rain, which seemed operated by a remote control, like in The Truman Show. The night sprinklers of the park had suddenly turned on, starting to spray water on the teenage couple during their first kiss.

We parted abruptly and started running towards the street. The grass turned into asphalt. Our kiss turned into a decisive laughter.

"What is this? Why are they using sprinklers in winter?" I was confused.

"It has been 2 months since it last rained here. Maybe that's why." Tommaso was always a rational guy.

"Or maybe it is Saint ... Remo. He might have wanted to send us a sign." I had inherited my father's DNA for pathetic puns. That genetic trait was so deeply rooted in our family that Doctor Innocenti would always churn out stupid puns – which he called "British humour" – even when, in his old age, he was suffering from Alzheimer's disease.

In any case, there was nothing to laugh about. My first potential kiss had been ruined by the sprinklers of a Ligurian village. *This happened because I am just cute*, I said to myself. *If I had been beautiful, it wouldn't have happened. If I had been wearing a Tampax, I would have kissed Tommaso. Two barely visible nipples cannot act like real tits.*

Tommaso looked entertained, with his male ability to forget, with his male ability to go on, with his male ability to shake his shoulders and say that everything is going to be fine.

I was beset by paranoia and by an inferiority complex, with my female inability to minimise, with my female inability to reject painful memories, with my female inability to push away overthinking and insecurities. Our kiss was over. It had never started, actually, because I didn't deserve it.

The last 30 minutes felt like the sequence of a silent movie, interrupted every now and then by black titles announcing the following scene. We were like black and white characters from a 1930s' film. Our movements were snappy and unnatural, as if there were a few frames missing.

The title of the scene of our encounter was "Destiny," the one with the ice-creams was "The Walk", while the title of the scene of our kiss should have been "The Disaster."

Tommaso rummaged in his pockets for a cigarette. He turned around and lit it up, protecting it from the wind with the back of his hand. "The Cigarette." Maybe that little burning thing was the end of our movie. Maybe we had, literally, burnt our bridges.

"Would you like a drag?" he asked me.

"No."

Everything had literally gone up in smoke.

# CHAPTER 13

## Dinosaurs

I wasn't a smoker. Maybe this is why after the cigarette, Tommaso had accompanied me back to my hotel and the whole story of the ice cream and the failed kiss under the weeping willow had shrunk, like a deflating balloon that dances awkwardly in the air and eventually dies in a small sack of non-biodegradable plastic.

The next day I went back home, and in the following days, at school, we only exchanged some sad "Hellos", tattooed over a grin. First the sprinklers (and then the cigarette) had flooded our love and then burned it to death, in a strange metaphorical subversion. The smoke, though, had followed me home: I was on duty for Doctor Innocenti's anti-cancer campaign. He had enlisted me as an activist to make students at the Liceo Scientifico Newton quit smoking.

"Everything clear?"

"Yes, Papà."

"Where did you put the stickers?"

"In my schoolbag."

"And the fliers?"

"In my diary."

"Thank you, honey. Good luck!"

Every year my father supported the "I kill" campaign, which aimed to discourage cigarette consumption in schools. That year, the Padua Anti-Cancer Association had distributed 1876 stickers with the image of a speaking dinosaur that said, "Smoking kills." The link between dinosaurs and cigarettes wasn't so clear to me, but the Association were certain that the prospect of receiving a free sticker to stick on one's scooter would have been an infallible deterrent against youth smoking.

So, I ended up distributing stickers outside my school with enthusiasm and devotion. A part of me was deeply convinced that dinosaurs could save the world. The other part, however, wondered how an extinct species was supposed to save the human race from extinction.

"Hey, guys, would you like a free sticker?"

I had never felt so dorky in my life. Like Giorgio Mastrota on mattress commercials on TV; there's nothing worse than a clever person who knows he is doing an extremely stupid thing. You can see the loss of dignity.

"Guys! Would you like a sticker?"

"I'll take 3."

Like drugs.

They were selling like hot cakes. They did all end up on scooters, though. On scooters of boys and girls who smoked. Lighting up a cigarette while riding scooters with stickers saying that 'smoking kills' made them feel cool. It was a form of rebellion. A challenge to the jinxing science.

"Guys, do you like dinosaurs?"

"Guys, throw those cigarettes away and read this!"

"Guys, do you have a minute?"

After I was suspended, I had been enjoying a decent reputation, but now I felt like an ethnic minority guy in a chicken uniform, distributing McChicken vouchers in front of a Mac Donald's in Times Square.

The love I felt for my father could be evaluated by the dizzying collapse of my style.

"Innocenti!"

Miss Sferzaferri suddenly appeared behind me.

"What are you doing here? Don't you know that it is illegal to distribute advertising material in front of the school?"

"I didn't know. Sorry. I'll stop," I apologised straight away.

"What is this for? A Take That concert?" She burst out laughing. Everybody knew about my obsession and couldn't come to terms with the fact that someone who was able to write in Latin prayed every night in front of a poster of 5 Mancunian boys who were struggling to write in their own language.

"No, Miss. This is for an anti-cancer campaign." I explained. Miss Sferzaferri was on her pink Graziella bike. She was holding the handlebars with one hand, using the other one to smoke her Merit. She had no hands left to grasp my stickers, so I put a few of them in the basket of her bike.

"It's an anti-smoking campaign." I added.

She started coughing as a sign of disapproval and I felt the need to say some more encouraging words. "It's for young people, Miss. You can carry on smoking."

The verbal diarrhea had struck again. In an attempt to make things better, I always made it worse. I suffered from a haemorrhage of unhappy sentences.

"The mascot is a dinosaur. You can give them to your daughter."

"What's the message, Innocenti?" She asked me skeptically.

"It says 'I kill.' It would be perfect for your daughter: she can't read yet!"

Miss Sferzaferri looked at me, like a doctor observing a patient affected by an unknown kind of psychosis. Her look was enquiring, but sympathetic.

"Well, helping your father is a noble thing to do; you're a good girl, Innocenti!"

She took the bundle of stickers and rode away on her bike trailing an invisible "Just Divorced" sign. She dashed along the cobblestones of Via Broletto, towards the porches, swaying past the students, the schoolbags and the lunchtime chats, which, she thought, compared to her life, were as futile as fairy floss.

"Miss!" My voice pretended to reach her before it was too late, but the volume was intentionally low, so she couldn't really hear me. "Riding on pavements is illegal too!"

The horde of high school students gradually scattered. It was 1:30 p.m. and the stinky Newton students were eager to go back home, where their mothers, grandmothers or housemaids had prepared pasta with Bolognese sauce, steak and mashed potatoes.

Seen from above, the lunchtime of a Paduan school looked like a stream of jeans, scooters and Invicta schoolbags, spreading in all directions at the ring of the bell, like blood pumped through the arteries, through the widespread system of porches and narrow streets covered in cobblestones, which made voices and noises rebound, turning Padua into a pretty loud mouthed town.

Gradually, the stream of students scattered through the bridges and the squares to the suburbs, past the city centre walls, in the lifts, beyond the house doors, to the laid tables. When televisions in the kitchens were turned on, the noise of the streets outside disappeared.

I was about to go home too, where my mother had prepared a dish of Costa & Catalogna, (the Venetian version of chicory and chard.) That's how I saw those boiled vegetables in my mind, like the title the 1970s TV show Starsky & Hutch. My mother used to buy those vegetables at the market in Piazza della Frutta. Costa was sweet, Catalogna was bitter, but they got along, especially in my mouth. They were a local produce. I was never able to find them again, anywhere in the world. Every time I think of Costa & Catalogna, I miss my mamma.

"Alice!"

Thinking about my love for vegetables, I had almost forgotten my teenage love. Tommaso.

"Why are you covered in dinosaurs?"

He had seen me from 500 metres away, while riding down Riviera Mussato on his scooter at 50 kilometres an hour and looking through his helmet visor. Probably I looked like a living tyrannosaurus.

"Are they so obvious? … I'm so embarrassed! It's for my father. He wants everybody to quit smoking to prevent cancer. Dinosaurs are supposed to convince them."

"Hahaha! That's so sweet of you. But why a dinosaur?"

"It has nothing to do with dinosaurs. It's an extinct species, so it should represent the danger of extinction. Maybe it implies the extinction of cigarettes. I don't know, Tommi."

I had just switched from Tommaso to Tommi without asking his permission. I had drastically narrowed the gap between us. Maybe I had finally found some courage.

"Alli, you're so crazy!" He had switched from Alice to Alli without asking my permission. He had drastically narrowed the gap between us. Maybe he was crazy.

"Let's skedaddle. I'll give you a ride."

*Let's skedaddle.* That expression sounded so old-fashioned to my ears. Maybe Tommaso's language had become extinct too, just like dinosaurs.

For one moment there I saw he was as dorky as I was. I mean, he was wearing glasses under the helmet visor! That was the image that had made me see him under a different light. The helmet itself was totally uncool. You could immediately spot those wearing a helmet. They looked like macro cephalic aliens.

Maybe he had read my mind, because he had stopped the engine and had taken the helmet off.

"Are you coming or not? I won't bite … I'm not a dinosaur."

And while he was lighting a cigarette, he once again became the second most beautiful man on earth to me. He had a new haircut and now he resembled "Tommaso" Cruise in Top Gun. Had he been shorter, everybody would have mistaken him for the Hollywood actor. His hair was sweaty and messy because of the helmet. He had taken his glasses off to look at me better and without seeing my imperfections. I, on the contrary, focused on his perfection. His inquiring eyes were as green as the sea of the Emerald Coast, his hands were tapered but strong, like a volleyball player, his nails were short, perfect, not bitten. There was no sign of stress-eaten cuticles. The skin on his knuckles was dry because of the cold weather, his teeth were perfectly white, and his lips were fleshy …

I was hypnotised. The ride would only have lasted a minute, because the school was very near my home, but I decided to make that minute significant. I grasped him tightly by his chest, like a monkey. I wanted to feel safe and to press my breasts against his back at the same time. My nipples were as hard as pins again and that heat between my legs forced me to get as close to him as possible. I could smell him inside the helmet, which he had offered to me, like a real gentleman. Some strange things were happening inside that helmet. First I had tried to lick its edges to taste Tommaso's saliva, in case there was some hint of it, had he sneezed in there. Then I had closed my eyes and imagined our kiss in Sanremo. How it could have been if it had happened. I had started kissing the helmet, pretending to kiss him. All the while hoping he couldn't see me in the rear-view mirror.

I ran my hands down his legs. I couldn't stop them. I wanted to touch him. I wanted to slip into his trousers and feel his heat. I wanted to caress that soft thing that turns into that hard thing that boys have behind the zip of their jeans.

I was horrified by myself, by those indecent thoughts that would have disappointed the spirit of Nonno Sergio. My heart was pounding in my chest and before my fingers could get closer to Hell, Tommaso took my hand inside his hand to protect it from the cold wind. I felt a bomb of light exploding in a million dazzling beams inside my heart, filling it with sweet honey. The famous skipping of the heartbeat.

We got home and I felt as if my childhood was fading away. Love, lust, passion. Maybe they were becoming more real than how I used to feel when looking at a poster or listening to a song.

As I rang the doorbell, Tommaso bolted away on his white horse named Vespa. Maybe he hadn't noticed anything. Maybe for him, that ride had been nothing but a cold, windy minute.

# CHAPTER 14

## Photographs

"1500 lire to extract the negatives. 500 for each print."

That was Mr Broncolato's business. He was the owner of the Broncolato o Rimborsato Photocompany Ltd on Via Zabarella. When he opened his photography and film development shop at the end of the 1970s, he couldn't have imagined that his career would have reached its peak between 1993 and 1997 thanks to Take That, two words he couldn't even pronounce.

"Dayk Dad!" he used to say. Thanks to those two simple, misspoken words, he had been able to pay off the mortgage for his suburban terrace house in just a few months.

It was the golden era for that kind of business, when photographic film was still the only way people could take photos, but at the same time the world was already beginning to be affected by a 'sharing' obsession. Had there been smartphones, in those years, Mr Broncolato wouldn't have made any money. But the old Nokias couldn't take pictures, and people still wanted to take pictures of their idols, bring those pictures to school, share them, show them off, sell them, resell them.

Mr Broncolato's business consisted of producing new negatives from videotapes, magazines and other original photographs. In his darkroom, he took pictures of pictures and stills from videotape frames. Then he developed the negatives to print new photographic copies of the originals. He had practically become a photographer.

The pictures and videotapes to manipulate came from concerts, newspapers and TV shows. If he could take a good picture, without the glare of the flash being visible, the final result could be as perfect as the original.

Many teenagers had drawers full of "original" pictures of Mark in front of Big Ben, or Robbie walking in his neighbourhood. They convinced themselves that they were the authors of those pictures. They believed they had actually been outside Robbie's house, or been invited by his mother for lunch. Maybe some of them dreamed about being in his bed. All sorts of stories sprang from the photographs. New friends and a new reputation sprang from those stories. Every picture gave us a bit more of self-confidence. It had all started as a forgery of dreams; later it became a market worth millions, with no boundaries. Someone had started selling those photographs, making people believe they were originals. "Would you like to buy a picture of Robbie in front of his house? It's 10,000 lire."

Forgers spiced the transactions with juicy details about the moment they had taken the pictures. You would end up believing those stories. Forged dreams multiplied. Anyone could show a picture of a Take That concert in Manchester without having ever been to England. Extracted photographs were like lies; they increased in number, copies of copies spreading in every direction and eventually being caught red-handed. "That picture is not original! I've seen it in a magazine! Give me my money back (bitch)!"

The only person who didn't suffer a loss from all of this was Mr Broncolato. Whether they were real or fake, he kept on developing negatives and printing copies. One day, at school, Broncolato junior made me an offer to join the family business: he asked me to let his father print my pictures and sell the copies directly. It was going to be a huge business for all of us, because my photographs were 100% authentic. I really had met Take That. I really had recorded 7 hours of concerts, car chases and hotel rooms, totalling 604,800 extractable frames. My pictures were clearly recognisable, like diamonds among zircons.

Eventually I let him convince me and my photos were displayed on the notice board of Broncolato o Rimborsato, each one with the date and the place where they had been taken and, of course, since I was the photographer, with my name printed on the back.

In a few months I had become a kind of celebrity and I had earned about 600,000 lire, without paying a cent to print them, since Mr Broncolato was taking a share of the profits. I had sold myself, for 600,000 lire. Maybe that was all I was worth, because on that notice board were pieces of my life. It was a mosaic of delirious fans and broken hearts. Fragments of my idol's eyes and smiles, taken in a rush. Pictures of muddy shoes, ripped jeans, trickling mascara and hands holding placards. Photos of opening gates, of legs running under a stage. Portraits of little men with insignificant jobs: bodyguards, taxi drivers, press agents. I had sold them too. Those little men; the ones who had helped us get front row seats at the concert or who had given us information on the hotels. Maybe those people had their own lives, crazy daughters like us, a wife cheating on them, a boss who exploited them. Their futile and mediocre existence had gained a dimension of authority for a short time.

Standing there, in front of that notice board, I felt powerful. Only a true fan could understand that in that collage there was a whole life; dreams of impossible, perfect and painful loves; a world where we were all sisters, daughters of a lesser god, who was probably Take That's manager.

"Congratulations. It's good to be young!" Mr Broncolato used to say, as I walked out of his shop with the money in my hands, a haul of 50,000 lire notes.

I wonder if only people who had lost their hair, like him, could say "It's good to be young" to a teenager, without being hated for it. There was nothing good in being a teenager, just tasks and prohibitions. Maybe youth could only be appreciated when you are old or excessively bald, like Mr Broncolato.

It was spring 1994. I had begun to wear my denim jacket, and there was a vanilla aroma in the air, because Caffè Cavour had started to make ice creams again. Summer was right around the corner and school was about to break up.

On the day of my 16th birthday, I was walking home with 16 photographs under my arm. They were the best of my 604,800 frames. Perhaps I should have been happy, because I was young, as Mr Broncolato said. Still I was deeply frustrated.

My panties were still bloodless. My hair was bushier under my armpits than under my skirt. My breasts were still barely visible under my shirt, like toys forgotten under the bed sheet. I had 600,000 lire to buy a fancy new dress, but I had already spent half of my money to buy bras of every size, cosmetics and tampons. I had accelerated my reality. I was pretending to be something I wasn't, because I didn't like who I was anymore.

"What are you going to do with all this stuff?" yelled my mother (starting to check my purchases) as soon as I got home.

"You know, you will never wear more than a small size bra! Don't think that your tits will be bigger than that. My chest was as flat as a pancake. What you see here has been made by a surgeon!" Then she burst out laughing, before vanishing behind the pages of *Novella Duemila* magazine.

Laura, her sisters, Matilda and a couple of schoolmates of mine were due to arrive at 8 p.m. There was going to be a cake, followed by a screening of the concert at Earls Court. I had decided to burn the pictures, instead of birthday candles. The cake was already in the living room, on the table in front of the television, with 16 photographs stuck in the whipped cream, each one representing a wish. I wanted to light them up one by one, then blow them out, maybe to make each wish come true.

My father was watching a Piero Angela documentary about mammals in New Zealand, as usual, in his tweed slippers, with his feet resting on the coffee table next to the cake.

My mother was in the kitchen, trying to remove the stains from the blue tiles on which my father had glued 45 English words, in order to make me memorise them during meals.

At half past 7 the doorbell rang. It was Laura's sisters, without Laura. Their mother had just been admitted to hospital after fainting at the Giotto shopping mall. Whatever the problem was, it was serious. Whatever the problem was, we needed to run to the hospital. They asked my father to come with us. Maybe the problem was more serious than I thought.

# CHAPTER 15

## Hospital

Tessa Islanda was a slender woman in her forties. She had a pale face, and timid blonde curls over her bony shoulders. She resembled a Moulin Rouge dancer, well-proportioned and sensual. Overall, she reminded me of a French beautician. Maybe it was her daintiness and her Genoese, almost Parisian accent, together with her taste for slightly eccentric clothes. The style of clothes that makes you think, "I like it, but not on me." Her nails were always perfect and covered with pearl pink nail polish, a colour that only beauticians and old ladies can wear without feeling embarrassed.

Laura was more like a rock n' roll version of her mother. In attempt to rebel, Laura had decided to wear short, black dyed hair and heaps of piercings. I was looking at her from the ward door on the eighth floor, east wing, of the Padua hospital. Tessa Islanda had left for the Island, a faraway place from where, they said, there was no way back.

I had always thought that you don't have cancer until they find out that you actually have it. One day you run happy and carefree across the wheat fields, the next you are the wheat that the harvesters reap. Tessa Islanda found out that she had a terminal liver cancer while she was buying ham and sage at the Giotto shopping mall. She had felt sick, bowed by a stabbing pain in her abdomen. She had fainted, they had called an ambulance, she had had an MRI. She had to leave the ham behind.

All this happened while I was trading Take That stickers and her daughter was listening to *Love Ain't Here Anymore*, eager to eat her mother's ham rolls. The seriousness of a situation must always be contextualised.

My father had already talked to the head oncologist: he *was* the head oncologist. And after a careful consideration of the test results, they confirmed that there was nothing they could do but palliative treatment, in order to slow down the course of the disease.

There were two vocabularies for me: the Italian one and the oncologist's one. I had been raised with the latter. Words and expressions I had heard my father say to his patients on the phone.

» "metastatic cancer";

» "tumour cell proliferation";

» "PET scan";

» "CT scan";

» "chemotherapy, radiotherapy";

» "immune response";

» "reactive protein";

» "carcinoma, sarcoma, melanoma";

» "treatment cycle, preventive surgery."

I had almost graduated in oncology, just by hearing him talk. He wanted me to become a doctor, and one day he had introduced me to a boy called Ezio. He was my age. Leg sarcoma. 2 months left to live. Because when you have cancer, your verdict is attached to your name, like personal data on a passport. You don't have cancer. Cancer has got you. My father just wanted me to talk to Ezio. Maybe he wanted me to understand how lucky I was. Maybe he wanted to see if I could manage the situation, if I had the guts. And my guts were upside down. I had ended up bonding with Ezio. I had bought him all the Take That CDs, I used to tell him what happened at school, and before the summer holidays, I had written him an affectionate letter. When Ezio smiled and told me that he felt lucky anyway, I would lock myself in the bathroom and cry. Then I would go back to him, pretending that nothing had happened. Ezio had died a few weeks later and his brother in law had called me to tell me that they had read my letter in the church, at the funeral.

I could never be an oncologist, but I had learned enough to understand that my father was right. Tessa Islanda's island was really too far away. I could tell that by the way doctors whispered, by the nurse's compassionate looks, by the man who carried the dinner who, peeking out from behind the door with a tray of boiled rice said, "I'm sorry, I'm sorry!" and stepped back immediately. It was clear that there were too many tubes attached to her body to offer a meal that needed to be eaten with cutlery.

Laura and I held each other for 10 minutes. When she saw me arrive at the hospital, she ran to me sobbing and clung to me tightly. We both cried. It was like the repeat of our running beyond the gates of San Siro, when for us, the fans, getting first in line to take the best spots, closer to the stage, was a matter of life or death. We always ran, Laura and I. We ran to get to an appointment on time, to take a train, to buy the first copy of *Cioè* magazine. We ran because when you are 16 you don't even know how to walk. This time, however, she was running faster than me. She wanted to pass me all her pain, as fast as she could, like a weight during a relay race. And after our embrace, her load was still too real, too heavy. She couldn't pass it to me. It was her turn, not mine.

"How is she?" I asked. Stupid question for a serious situation.

"They have sedated her. They haven't told her yet how bad it is. My father has gone home to fetch her some clothes. Happy birthday, by the way." She even managed to smile, thinking about how ironic all that was. "I was hoping to sing *Happy Birthday* to you, tonight … now I guess you have to wish me good luck instead."

"Try not to be so pessimistic now. My father is consulting with his colleagues. They will do everything they can. You trust him, don't you? At least your mother is in good hands." I was talking like the president of the United States who, while enemies are bombing the White House, keeps on saying "Don't worry. Everything is under control. The National Guard has been alerted. They are going to rescue us." I was like a second-class actor playing the role of senator, lawyer or governor in a B-movie.

"I trust your father. I really do. It's just that we are so upset. She's never been sick. Never. She doesn't smoke, she doesn't drink, she exercises. I can't believe it. Do you know what I mean? If we had only noticed it earlier!"

From the moment they had found out about their mother's disease, Laura and her sister had started reviewing all the moments spent with her in the last 5 years, rummaging through the memories to find a detail, a clue, a sign of the disease that they might have ignored.

"Do you remember 3 years ago, in Palermo, when she fainted in the heat?"

We should have realised.

"She had been telling me for a year that wine nauseated her …"

We should have realised.

"One day, she looked much paler than usual, almost yellow …"

We should have realised.

They were looking for a reason to feel guilty, a confession they needed to give meaning to their pain. In order to accept such terrible news, they needed to find an explanation at least. If they had noticed that something was wrong before, maybe their mother could have been cured. If they hadn't been so ignorant and selfish, there would have been time to save her.

I recognised that. I had seen it happen before. When cancer struck, the first reaction was always incredulity, as if they had forgotten human beings were born with an expiry date; the surprise of not being immortal, followed by fear. Fear of death. So real and primordial. Fear of leaving their loved ones to their fate. Concern for their children. Regret for not being able to see them become adults. Anger. Anger for the time that is snatched from them, almost without notice.

The painful truth of cancer was right in that word, "almost". Because it was one thing to die without notice, for example in a car crash, but another thing altogether to receive advanced notice. Short notice, of course- sometimes very short- but however received, it gave you time to regret your choices, to curse your mistakes, to think of the "ifs" and the "maybes".

After reviewing all the emotions, the last feeling was always serene acceptance. The will to live the last months to the fullest. Days began to be filled with love. Not just for family and friends; love for the world. The sun, the sky, the walks, the music, the sea, the candies. Love for the little things. Walking, breathing, eating, seeing. It was as if, growing up with my father, I had already had a run-through. If something like that had happened to me, I would have known what to expect. But I had been lucky. It was never my turn. It was never our turn. It was like musical chairs. When the music stopped, I always found myself sitting. I wondered why. I asked my dad too.

"Why did it happen to them and not to us?"

The answer was always "I don't know." No matter how much science there was behind cancer, it was always "Fate" that determined how things were supposed to happen. That's why I was a hypochondriac. If I couldn't control my destiny with good habits — eating healthy food, no alcohol, no cigarettes, no drugs — then I could have been affected by some disease at any time and without a reason!

How could I live like this, knowing that I could be dead the next day? This sense of uncertainty had made me anxious to live. I wanted it all, and all at once. Nothing was impossible. "Let's do it now and not tomorrow." But also, "I have a pain in my arm. What can it be?" "Look at this mole, Papá. Is it dangerous?"

I tried not to think about those things. I chased my anxiety away, because now Laura needed me, and I had to reassure her, just like I used to do with the patients who called my father at home. What I would have liked to say was "It's completely normal that you have cancer. Everybody gets it sooner or later, even people doing all the right things." Instead, what I said was always "You are so unlucky. I wonder why you, among all the people on Earth. It's a shame that these things happen to the best people."

The first thing they wanted to hear was that they had been unlucky. They needed the doctor to admit it. After that, they could go on and talk about treatments and life expectancy. By that point, they would stop hoping and start calling on science. However, I couldn't forget what I knew; namely, that in the end, "Fate" was always the boss.

"You'll see. With the right treatment, she will get well soon." I told my friend a lie. Then I held her hands, I looked at her in the eyes and I told her the truth: "This reminds us that we must live every day as if it were our last day."

Laura answered immediately, as if she wanted to reproach me. "That's what we are already doing, isn't it? We are two crazy girls and we must stay crazy till the end. I don't want to die normal."

She was right. We were already doing that. Living our days to the fullest, like two crazy girls. Dreaming impossible dreams, pursuing pipe dreams, with the wind in our hair.

"How is it going with Tommaso?" she asked me.

"He gave me a lift home a few days ago, but I kept on thinking of Gary!" I gave a hint of a smile. Perhaps I knew I was lying. "We are just friends. Why would he care about a girl like me?"

"Stop it! You pretend to be tough, but I know you like him! Kiss me! Kiss me!" She was touching her lips mocking me kissing him.

"I'd rather die!"

Silence. I felt terribly bad for saying that word. It was really inappropriate. Laura stared at me for a second and then we burst out laughing. The fat head nurse wearing Dr. Scholl's clogs hushed us. As soon as she turned around, we burst out laughing again, covering our mouths with our hands.

It was dark outside. They turned the lights on in the ward. And as we laughed, we started crying. We cried harder than we had ever laughed. We needed no words. The tears of two sisters were eloquent enough.

"*All I do each night is pray, hoping that I'll be a part of you again someday,*" Laura started singing *Pray*, and I joined her. Maybe praying was the only reasonable thing to do, when you had lost your faith in science and destiny.

The head nurse peeked out to hush us again, because singing was not allowed in the hospital, but then she stopped in the doorway. She knew that song. We were allowed to pray. She smiled at us and went back to her office.

# CHAPTER 16

## Summer Music Festival

During his long career, my father had taken care – more or less successfully – of a parade of celebrities, from all sectors. From religion to pornography; bishops, archbishops, singers, ministers, rich businessmen, strippers. Considering the nature of his job, though, he often didn't keep in touch with his patients. Only half of them usually survived, and if one wanted to take advantage of the association – for example, to be blessed by a religious man – they had to do it rapidly. Like when my father woke me up in the middle of the night and took me – still wearing my pyjamas – to the bishop's house, inside the Padua Cathedral. When we entered the dying bishop's bedroom, I was still in my slippers. The bishop was wearing white clothes, as white as his face, pale as anything. My father made me lean toward him. The man whispered something religious in my ear and touched my head with his hand. That gesture must have been an extraordinary effort for him, maybe the last one before passing away.

I only remember his tender look and his grey, watery eyes. When death arrives, it is as if the colours of the iris and the pupils melt in a decomposing soup.

Another time, he introduced me to the president of the most important Italian bank. I was only 11 years old, but it was never too soon to start looking for a job. I was welcomed by men wearing ties and leather shoes. I was offered Gianduiotti chocolates and asked if I was good at maths. The president had assured me that there would be a job for me in high finance in 10 years' time. Unfortunately, he died a year later, so I wasn't forced to study economics at university.

My father wasn't an insensitive man. It was just that after having seen so many people die, he got used to it. He didn't see his patients as virtuous saints to feel sorry for, but as normal people with all their flaws. He treated them the same he would have treated healthy people, but with less haste.

"Alice." When he called me by my full name, he was about to tell me either incredible or terrible news. "What's in the camera?"

I got it. Maybe my father had decided to take his camera back after taking an intensive filmmaking course at the University of the Third Age.

"Do you mean apart from the videos with Mamma making gnocchi and me drawing shadows with my quill pen?"

"Don't be sarcastic. It's important."

"You don't have the right to take it away from me! It's a present!" *If you don't know whose fault it is, the fault is always yours, Alice. Use your defensive strategy.*

"Don't be silly. I've just asked you to tell me what's recorded in it. Don't snarl at me like your mother. Just answer my question."

"OK … there are a few videos of Take That, Montecarlo, Sanremo and some other adventures of mine. Trains, concerts, car chases. Mostly Laura and me. Nothing you would be interested in, Papà."

"You're wrong, my dear."

I knew that expression. I used to call it "the fifth smile". My father had different smiles. The first one meant he was happy. The second one was the smile you fake before taking a picture or when you are having a conversation with someone you can't stand, but you pretend to be intrigued. The third smile was the paternal, tender and compliant one. The fourth smile, which I noticed in a very few occasions, was the sexual one, when he was on "predator mode" and stared at Mamma or at some nurse with his penetrating eyes. The fifth smile was the satisfaction-for-imminent-victory one. The smile of omniscience. The smile of writers or movie producers after the shooting is over. The smile of a person who has a plan in mind and knows how things will end and is about to share it with someone who is completely unaware of what is going on; the smile of a scientist who has just won the Nobel Prize and is about to tell his wife.

"I have a new patient. Liver carcinoma. His name is Raimondo Merletti. Does it sound familiar?"

"Raimondo Merletti? *That* Raimondo Merletti?"

My father's fifth smile was enjoying my first smile. The happiness smile.

"Yes. The executive director of the Summer Music Festival!"

I started jumping up and down all over our living room, kissing and hugging Doctor Innocenti, who pretended to smarten himself up, shooing me away with his hands, like you do with flies.

"Will Take That be there? When? When? When?"

I was screaming, singing, jumping. If my father was omniscient, I felt omnipotent.

"Raimondo told me that he will get you 2 backstage passes for the 22nd of June episode, in Pula, Croatia, when Take That perform at the Festival."

"I love you so much, Papà! Thank you, thank you, thank you!" Hug delirium, stream of consciousness, hypomania … the symptoms of joy.

"What's all this racket?" The Tiger of Bengal appeared, interrupting any expression of happiness.

"Mamma, I'm going to the Summer Music Festival to meet Take That!"

"Oh, finally! But after that, you'll have to stop acting like a child. You are 16 now."

"Yes, but until I menstruate, I can be a child as long as I like." I glanced at my father with a conspiratorial look. He was trying not to laugh. My mother, as usual, had not grasped the irony of my words, and now she was ruminating. She was in her "break from herself" mode.

After a few seconds, without being able to draw any conclusion, she added, "It makes no sense. You and your bullshit!" She retreated to the kitchen in a snit and slammed the glass door to highlight her annoyance.

I perfectly recall what I was wearing that day and my exact spot on the stage of life, as you do when something really important happens. I was wearing a strapless white dress with red flowers, my hair was still wet because I had been caught in the spring rain in via San Pietro. In addition, I had a hint of lip-gloss and a purple, bitter nail polish, which was supposed to help me quit biting my nails. I kept that dress for the next 25 years. I was superstitious.

As for the spot, my father was sitting on the blue sofa with tulips and I was standing on the 15 million lire Persian rug, next to the cactus, which was a present from the accountant, and which kept stinging me in the arm every time I exulted.

It was one of those moments you want to remember forever. It's destiny. It's cancer. You can call it whatever you want. *Whatever it is, Gary, nothing will keep us apart!*

"There's more."

My father had let me vent my elation, absorb the impact and assimilate the news. It was more or less the same thing he used to do with his patients when he told them how many months they had left to live.

There was always a reaction period to be taken into account.

"What, Papà?" I asked, with my eyes and my mouth wide open, as if someone was stretching my skin with elastic bands.

"Raimondo also asked me if you would be interested in doing an internship next summer."

I kneeled down out of devotion, like when you receive a present that is so big that you cannot accept, but that it is also impossible to refuse.

"They are looking for young smart people who know everything about those silly things you watch on the TV music channel. I told him that you are fluent in English. I don't know whether they will ask you to make photocopies, move chairs or shoot videos, but they asked me if you can use a camera."

Fear. Disappointment. Inferiority complex. Invasive insecurity.

"Papá, I can't do anything with a camera but filming. Will they give me the pass even though I can't do anything?"

114

All of a sudden, I saw all my hopes fading away. The hot-air balloon was in danger. Soon a pelican would fly into it, making a hole in it. It would have fallen to the ground. I would have fallen too. From 7th heaven to a graveyard of dreams.

"Don't be as dramatic as your mother! Of course, they will give you the pass. With that cancer of his, he will give you 2 passes. But being an advanced stage of cancer with hepatic metastases, if you want a career in television, you have to make the most of this opportunity now. Raimondo has barely 6 months left to live."

My father could seem ruthless, but he wasn't, I swear. It was just that in his world, people walked with invisible labels with the expiry date on them. In his world, almost everyone had a time limit, like characters of a videogame. What was he supposed to do? Cut them out of his life and relegate them to the status of guinea pigs, or treat them as normal human beings and interact with them, as he would have done with people in good health, talking about work and opportunities, asking for favours and doing favours? At the end of the day my father saved lives, so he was entitled to ask for some concessions. Moreover, his patients adored him and kept buying him presents, like they did with Christmas cards. It was their way to avoid their tragic destiny. What they did with him was the same thing believers do with saints, when they light a votive candle or donate to the church. They prayed. They hoped.

"If you still have that video you recorded with my camera, with some background music, like those bungles you watch on MTV, give it to me and I'll hand it to Amanda, the secretary. They're not expecting a Steven Spielberg movie, don't worry!"

My father loved to laugh at his own jokes. Typical of someone who can't make other people laugh.

"OK, I have the videos with Take That, but they need to be edited ..." I thought, biting the cuticles of my left thumb with my eyes closed.

"Stop biting your nails! You are a woman now!" My father pulled my hand away from my mouth. The nail biting made him really angry, more than anything else, like failure at school or a criminal act.

I was walking back and forth. "I need to edit them … and there's no music …"

I had an epiphany.

"I need an editor!"

A strange smile had appeared on my face, halfway between number 1 and number 4.

"I know someone who can help me! Sorry, Papà, I need to make a phone call."

I gave him a quick kiss and left.

# CHAPTER 17

## Music

I had no doubt about the person I wanted to come with me to the Summer Music Festival. I called Laura as soon as my father told me the news. My mother allowed me a 3 minute, 45 second telephone call because she had made risotto with porcini mushrooms and she and my father were waiting for me at the table. Five seconds had been enough to communicate the message. For the other 3 minutes and 40 seconds there were screams of happiness, swear words, liberation, threatening, temporary and contradictory expressions. The general sense of the call was "So there is a god in this world."

Laura was in the middle of the worst tragedy a child could live – the death of their mother – and welcomed the news as "the minimum that life can give me to compensate for all my pain", but also "luckily I have some friends" and "when I marry Robbie, all this will make sense."

When she hung up, she ran to her mother, yelling out of joy.

"I'm so happy for you!" Tessa said. *Forgive me if I won't be able to pick you up at the gate this time,* she added in her mind.

Laura felt sad afterwards. How could she be so insensitive as to be happy in front of her mother? During the last weeks she had forgotten what smiling meant. She couldn't remember how unexpected and simple happiness was. Sadness was laborious, like a tired dog you have to keep on a leash all day long. An old dog that doesn't tolerate noises, cold weather and long walks. An old dog that doesn't bark anymore.

Every afternoon Laura would sit next to her mother, and together they would leaf through old pictures. It was as if Tessa had resigned herself to death and tried to remember how she was when she was still alive.

"Look at me here. I was in a really good shape! We were in Umbria, your father and I. That red dress was a present from him," she said with her eyes half-closed, while a sweet dream took her back to the past. When she opened her eyes, she looked at the young Tessa of the picture and silently asked her, "Would you have ever imagined dying so young?" Those words sounded like a reproach. But the young Tessa silently replied, "You are not dead yet! And you still have the red dress."

After that, Tessa decided she would start wearing that dress again, and she forced herself to take long walks in the sunlight. She started putting makeup on again, going to the cinema and to the pastry shop to buy cream horns, which she hadn't eaten for 40 years, since she had always been on a diet. She decided that she would do only pleasant things, until the end of her days.

Every day she asked to be photographed, so she could add new pictures to the album and one day, looking at those pictures, someone would say "Look how happy Tessa was!"

Every now and then, she used to come to my father's office and Laura would come and "play" in my bedroom, as my mother obstinately insisted on calling it. In that period, all Take That songs acquired a brand-new meaning. We listened carefully to the words in order to repeat them to Tessa to support her in her fight against cancer. I even imagined what song they could have played at the funeral, but I never talked about that.

As teenagers, we had a true talent for drama. We were the best when it came to exaggerating and overdramatising feelings, which, in the case of a tragedy, was an essential gift you needed to have. We almost succeeded in wrapping up the entire situation in a song, and we cried listening to it. We also found an explanation in it, maybe peace, maybe an ending, maybe resignation.

Laura was preparing herself for the worst, but the worst was the sound of a pipe organ resonating in the endless sky. Music was our blood, in those years of shared headphones on a scooter, when the only sound you could hear was the wind in your ears; in those years, when you raised the volume to drown out the screaming protests from the universe of your bedroom; in those years, when music measured time. It measured the afternoons spent watching MTV, the homework at your desk, the trips in Papá's car. In those years, when music determined where you would have lived, in an endless pilgrimage towards an idol. Manchester, Seattle, New York; in those years, when music was the soundtrack of your death, the tune that everybody imagined for their own funeral.

In those years, we could live on music and explain the world with music. We could believe, love, and die with music inside us.

The day after the Great News, I was sitting in the classroom as if I had already got a job. I had just received a very low mark in Physics – that wouldn't influence my average grade, though – and I was almost happy. According to thermodynamics, energy can neither be created nor destroyed, but it can only be transformed. And I was transforming into Gary's future wife, with a job in the television industry. It wasn't important that thermodynamics had been eclipsed by Einstein's relativity.

"Innocenti! Stand up and come here."

At the last English oral test, the teacher had given me a meagre pass mark, because when I was talking about Coleridge's Kubla Kahn I had mentioned the last video by Soundgarden, *Black Hole Sun*, where the world melted down like in Coleridge's hallucination. Mr Quantini didn't watch MTV, so he had to trust my words, but he wasn't impressed.

On that worst day of my school career, I felt professionally successful. That day I realised that school grades don't matter in real life. The only thing that mattered was convincing Tommaso to edit my video.

When the recess bell rang, I rushed outside the classroom. For the occasion, I had put back on my lucky white floral dress. Tommaso didn't embarrass me anymore. He was just a device, a tool to get what I really wanted: Gary.

During an emergency, things acquire or lose importance. And he had lost it. The doors of my classroom opened and started spewing out ripped jeans, army jackets, floral skirts, crisp packets, wafts of dirty armpits, cigarettes and strawberry chewing gum.

I was a bit excited to see Tommaso again. The last time we had talked was when he given me a ride on his scooter, and I was afraid that the reason we hadn't spoken again was that he had caught me. He had felt that I liked him, that my heart was pounding, that my hand had gone close to the zip of his jeans. The right thing to do was to disappear, in order to let every suspicion evaporate, so I had disappeared from his radar for a while.

"Alice Innocenti!"

I had been downgraded. From Alli to Alice. From Alice to Alice Innocenti.

"Where have you been? Do you still remember my name?"

Unfortunately for me, I still remembered his name. Unfortunately for me, he was still gorgeous.

"What happened to your glasses?" He wasn't wearing them. Maybe he hadn't seen me distinctly. That's why he had called me by my full name, to be sure I was the right person.

"I wear contact lenses now. How are you?"

Tommaso always acted as if he were happy to see me. Maybe it was a strategy or a form of politeness. I couldn't believe he was really happy. The smile upon his face was still the number 1 smile. The happy smile, but it could have been smile number 2 as well. The fake smile.

He had a green t-shirt with a picture of Kurt Cobain, khaki army trousers and white Converse shoes that had turned grey.

"Cigarette?"

Without waiting for an answer, he signalled me to follow him to the courtyard. He crawled through the school corridors as if someone had just got him out of bed, as lazy as when he walked from his bedroom to the kitchen to have breakfast. He walked as if he didn't care about what was happening to the rest of the world, but he looked at me as if he cared about me. I was a few steps behind him, and he turned around to make sure I didn't get lost. My objective had been to use him as a mere tool for my professional activity. But now my pulse accelerated, and I was feeling nervous. Normally he was the one of few words and I was the one supposed to break the silence. But I was petrified.

So, from the classroom to the courtyard, what we had was just fragmented small talk.

"You look great in your summer clothes."

"Thanks. This dress has been in my wardrobe for years."

"Does it still fit you?"

*Here we go.* The comment that reminded me that yes, the clothes I had bought when I was 12 years old still fit me, because I hadn't grown up so much. Those words made me blush.

He lit a cigarette. "Tell me then. Why are we here?" He already knew everything. "Well, you don't show up outside my classroom every day, do you? What's on your mind?"

I felt everybody's eyes on us. In the chaos of chewed crisps and recess gossip, I was aware that the rest of the school was looking at us. Tommaso was a much-desired boy, maybe in the top 3 ranked of the most beautiful, intelligent, fearless students in Liceo Scientifico Newton. It was like I was interviewing God and I had only a few seconds at my disposal.

I braced myself and told him everything, starting from the job I could offer him if he helped me. A promise I couldn't really keep, but I trusted thermodynamics.

"OK, no problem. I'll help you with your video. Would you like to come by around 6?"

Was it so easy?

It was so easy.

"Perfect. I can't wait. Thank you, Tommi."

It was an affectionate, impulsive, sincere "Tommi".

Once the interview with God was over, I ran back to my classroom to get ready for the Latin test. I got another bad mark, confirming that that day of May 1994 was the negative peak of my school career.

I really needed to find a job.

# CHAPTER 18

## The Editor

At 6:05 p.m. I was at the door. I had arrived at 5:45 p.m. actually, but I preferred to wait for a few minutes. In other words, I had arrived early to make sure I would be late. It was one of Nonna Tilda's theories: *a woman should never finish what's on her plate and should always be late.* She believed in etiquette more than she believed in God. As a result, she was super skinny and managed to upset whoever she had an appointment with.

I rang the bell. It was a detached house in Palestro district. I had never been there, but it was clear that it was a fancy, middle class house. Tommaso's father was an entrepreneur from Trieste. He traded furniture and was often in Friuli for long periods. Tommi was an only child and he lived with his mother, waiting for his father to come back home from his long weekly trips.

The gate opened over a small yard. He was waiting for me at the door, in his pyjamas. I was still wearing the same dress. I didn't want him to think that I had smartened myself up for him.

"Are you wearing pyjamas?" I was trying to make him feel as embarrassed as I was.

"It's an Adidas tracksuit, actually, but thank you anyway!"

"I must have been misled by your slippers, sorry."

"Come inside. My mother isn't here. She'll be back after dinner."

Panic.

After my interview with God, Heaven's door had just been opened for me. As usual, however, I felt completely inadequate. Moreover, the fact that there were no adults around, keeping an eye on us, made me nervous.

Tommi led me straight to his bedroom, which, unlike mine, didn't have any Take That posters, but just a few pictures of

122

Nirvana, a framed photograph of Pearl Jam and a blue lava lamp on the nightstand. There were lots of blue things in that room:

» blue curtains;

» blue bedcover;

» blue rug;

» blue lamp.

"Do you like blue?"

"Hahaha! No. My mother does. Take a pew. You can put your bag on the bed, if you like."

"Take a pew." Such an old expression, almost ridiculous. I wondered if I had ever used those words to invite someone to sit down. Once again, he sounded far too polite to me, as if he were older than he actually was. I used to get side-tracked by the weirdest thoughts.

"You can sit here, next to me."

I was next to God now, therefore I was Archangel Gabriel, or, alternatively, Saint Peter.

"Wow! You have a brilliant computer!"

"It's a Mac. You don't see many of them around. It has special programs that I use for my stuff. Did you bring the video? We need to upload it."

"Of course. Here it is."

Our hands slightly touched when I handed him the tape and the scooter syndrome savaged me again.

"Look, Tommi … I still haven't seen it, and I haven't shown it to anyone. Please don't judge me. I feel such like a loser right now."

"Hahaha! You should feel like a loser! Do you have any idea how much fun I will make of you after watching six hours of you chasing Take That?"

"Idiot!"

I grabbed a pillow and threw it at him.

"Wait, let me upload this!"

The Mac started sucking images in. From that moment onward, there was no way back.

"Would you like a coke? It's still going to take about 30 minutes."

"Yes, please."

Tommaso went to the kitchen and I stopped and stared at my video appearing on the screen. I understand what they mean when they say that your life flashes before your eyes when you die. Maybe I was really in Heaven.

I could see the faces of all the members of Take That. There was the night run in Monte Carlo. The camera still on after falling to the ground. Our hands waving in front of the stage in Sanremo. Laura's tears. Our shoes touching each other in some train station or another. Slices of sky and trees passing by as the train ran fast. My smile casually filmed.

I suddenly felt an unlimited tenderness for Alice. It was as if, by putting her in a computer, she had become another person. Different from me. A fictional character of a fictional story, which probably once, had belonged to me, but that I was now watching like you watch a movie at the cinema. A movie that becomes your favourite, and you keep renting it from Blockbuster.

It was there. In that computer. The difference between real and ideal world. It was as if the only way to see the difference between them was making a Mac separate them.

"How long do we have left?" I asked. Tommaso came back with a coke and started checking the computer. *How long is it going to take? Once the files have been uploaded, will my real life still be important?* I wondered. I was confused and sad. I had an overwhelming desire to be sucked in by the computer, to keep living inside my dreams.

Tommaso started clicking something on the keyboard. I saw him selecting icons, cutting, adjusting sequences. Half an hour had already gone, and I didn't want to bother him, so I sat on his bed and started reading the lyrics inside the Pearl Jam CDs.

I felt comfortable in his bedroom. It smelled like tanned skin and talcum powder. A mix between a salty aroma and a sweet perfume. The smell of a person who has sweated on a sunny beach and has dried off with a towel before applying moisturising cream. Every now and then, I heard him sigh when he made a mistake and had to start all over again, but all in all he was so quiet, he could have been asleep. It had to be this way. I wished I could sleep with him, hug him, and snore blissfully on his chest without being judged. Before I knew it, I closed my eyes and while dreaming about sleeping with him, I fell asleep.

In my dream I was in Tuscany at Nonna Tilda's. I was wearing the same floral dress that I was wearing right then. Carmela and Ruggero were there, along with other guys I had never seen before (except maybe in a TV series I had watched with my mother and that my brain cells had joined in my dream.) We were riding our bikes, speeding through the wheat fields at sunset. We were riding fast, towards the sun. I could see my silhouette against the light. We were happy. My breasts had grown, so I was a signorina in the dream.

I was standing up on the bike, riding out of the saddle, like an expert. I was self-confident, radiant and beautiful. There was a boy riding behind me. In the dream I could only see his shoulders and his head from behind. Another silhouette standing out against the sunset. He reached me and we crashed. We fell down and started laughing, rolling over in the wheat field. I was on my back looking at the sky and he was above me. We stopped laughing and he looked me in the eyes as if he loved me. He lifted up my face towards his lips while his hands moved quickly down my legs, hesitantly and respectfully, but eager to touch me.

The boy was Tommaso.

I suddenly opened my eyes. He was next to me, on the bed.

"You're beautiful when you sleep. It's time to finish what we started ..."

So, halfway between dream and reality, Alice had her first kiss on May 24th, 1994 and found out that some romantic sentiments feel a lot like semi-sleep.

It was a long, slow, passionate kiss. Tommaso had started touching my lips with his, running his fingers through my hair, then he clung to me vigorously, so our tongues found each other. I didn't want to stop. When his hands slid on my tiny nipples, I let him. When he started wheezing and slipped his fingers between my legs, I let him, because I liked it. I didn't want him to stop. I wanted him to get in there, where it was all warm and wet, and I wanted to keep feeling that soft part of him that now was so hard and was pushing against my stomach. And I suddenly wondered if it was more of a sin because I wasn't a signorina. I pushed him away. He drew back immediately.

"I'm sorry, Alli. You're right. Too soon. Too fast. It's just that it's not easy to resist you."

I smiled at him. Every part of me was smiling at him, actually. My eyes, my nipples, the crack between my legs. But most of all, my heart. I was wondering, for the first time in a year, if he was the man I truly loved and not Gary.

Tommaso put himself back together quickly and went back to his computer. We started talking non-stop, to conceal our awkwardness. We were spewing words without any logic, because what was important was quantity. Every word was a step further away from that situation.

"How's the upload going?"

"Let me check."

"Good. Do it."

"Yes, no problem."

"Thank you."

"You're welcome."

"Keep me posted."

"Sure."

After a few words, we had changed direction and left that awkward event behind us. We were magically in sync again, to use an editing term.

"I've finished! I've cut a few scenes and put some background music in while you were sleeping."

"What music?"

"I'm not going to tell you. It's a surprise. You can watch it at home if you want."

"I hope it's Take That! You can't put Nirvana in a video with Take That!"

We burst out laughing and I was compelled to move my chair closer to him and intertwine my fingers with his. He turned towards me and took my face in his hands before kissing me. We repeated our passionate kiss. He started wheezing again and I pushed him away, saying that it was late, and I had to go home.

We stood up, he gave me the video and we both sighed, like at the end of an exhausting mountain trip, when you're breathless but incredibly happy and proud of yourself. A sigh to release our endorphins.

"Wait! We need to stick a label on it. They're in the left drawer. Can you get one for me?"

Tommaso rushed to the bathroom. There were 3 drawers on the left so I didn't know which one he was referring to. I started from the middle one and I pulled it open. Among a stapler and a few pens there was a picture. My heart stopped for a second. It was Tommi in the picture, and a brunette kissing him. There was a note on the photo in a marker pen, "I Love You Tommi" and a date on the back. It was from the week before.

Tommaso came back into his room and saw me holding the picture with my eyes full of tears. Not pouring down my face, rather more like conjunctivitis. Unexpressed, painful, restrained.

I looked at him with disdain and the scene turned into the sequence in a horror movie, where the character runs through rooms and corridors, with a thrilling music in the background, like in The Shining.

The imaginary camera operator walked backwards as I ran towards him, along the corridor, between Tommaso's room and the doorway. I was fast, I was running away from him. Tommaso ran after me, together with his excuses, like the Doppler Effect.

"Alli! Wait! It's not what it looks like! I haven't seen her in months! She's Canadian … Fuck! Alli, Wait!"

"I don't want my damned videotape anymore. Keep it!"

The corridor was long, the characters mistakenly entered the kitchen and the living room, before they could find the exit.

"I told you that I met her months ago. It was Christmas and I was on a study trip! Alli, I don't fucking care about her!"

The camera operator stopped at the doorstep with the characters. It was a low angle shot.

"Are you kidding me? Why did she write "I Love You" only a week ago then? Keep the videotape!"

*Throw the tape to the ground, Alice. Turn around and go away, Alice. Turn around and go back to the only man who can't make you suffer. Go back to the poster in your room.*

# CHAPTER 19

## The School Report

In Padua you knew it was summertime because of mosquitos. The Bacchiglione River would become an insect factory, and it seemed that the entire Po valley, the paddy fields near Rovigo, the Brenta River swamplands and the Venetian Lagoon would start to produce fiercer and fiercer beasts, willing to spoil our summer holidays.

Nevertheless, the first buzz, although annoying, would indicate the end of the school year. It was just a matter of days. You could count them down just like you counted mosquitos swatted on the wall, in an inversely proportional way. The more blood-stains on the ceiling, the fewer school days left. Basically, when your room looked like Picasso's Guernica, you were free. Trees would cover themselves with leaves, people started to go out more and the scooters speeding up on the night streets sounded almost drunk, like they had too much petrol to drink.

Ice-cream parlours would be open until midnight and naked thighs would abound in the squares. Your best friend would pick you up to go to Sottomarina because there was no more school. On the way to the city centre, you would stop by Ricordi's to buy summer CDs. On a Sunday night you would go and eat pizza on the rooftop at Stecca's. You would sleep until 10 in the morning, and at midday, you would go and sweat on a deck chair on the lawn of the Nuoto Duemila pool. Mothers and fathers would plan trips, whereas you would plan your days as if all of a sudden you had nothing to do for the rest of your life. Summer holidays would last 3 months, but it seemed like forever.

On that day in June 1994 I was staring at the 2 passes for the Summer Music Festival, which represented the entire future of my existence. Two yellow badges with blue contours and daisies – the emblem of the festival – on the background. There was my name printed on it. "Alice Innocenti". It was like a birth certificate. I only existed when I read my name on that pass. They had even duplicated me; on the second badge not only was there my name, but also the word "Guest". Not only did I have access to the backstage area, but I was allowed to bring a guest. I felt important.

My father was disappointed with what had happened with the video. He had been expecting to receive a copy to be sent to the festival's editorial staff, but his daughter had come back empty-handed. Then I had told him the truth, namely that I had given my first kiss to a boy who was hiding a picture of another girl in his drawer. Thinking about what I had just told him, he had caressed my head and sighed in disapproval. Then he had felt the need to console me with a series of paternal trivialities:

» "It doesn't matter. We'll think about it later."

» "These things happen, and they happen because you've become a woman."

» "He will regret what he has lost."

» "There are a thousand boys better than him!"

» "If I see him, I'll teach him a lesson."

Then he had concluded with his usual self-humour, that only made *him* laugh.

"I'll take you to Switzerland. If Gary doesn't fall in love with you at the festival, we'll find a new cow-milker!"

Maybe Switzerland was really what my father wanted for me. It was what every parent wishes for their own daughter. A safe and quiet place, with no surprises. A risk-free place, where it's hard to make mistakes and impossible to suffer.

"Nobody here wants to go to Switzerland, Papá." Let alone me, given that I had a ticket to go to Pula.

That day I went to school to collect my school report. Broncolato had given me a voucher to develop films at his father's shop, as a reward for helping him with his Latin translations. I had saved him from failing the year.

Matilda, however, had failed the year and had sent her mother to school in order to bribe her teachers with Hermes bags.

My mother came with me to read my results. There had been no surprises. High marks in all subjects, even in maths. They probably hadn't wanted to spoil my average grade.

"Well done, sweetheart!" Mamma kissed and hugged me in front of the headmaster's office. Around her, there was a coming and going of teachers and students whom she had never seen before, because she had never been to a parent-teacher meeting. The year-end school report was the only connection my mother had with my school life. There was her own destiny written on those papers: the destiny of an absent mother. With a brilliant report like that, she felt entitled to continue her absence during the following year, knowing that I didn't need help. It made her dance with joy, because her lack of responsibility had just been renewed.

"I'll rush home to tell your dad!"

Those were my only moments of glory with my mother.

I wondered if I would ever see Tommaso again. We hadn't talked since our first and last kiss. I saw him laughing in the yard with his friends and I decided to stay away from him. When I looked up to see if he was still there, I noticed that he was staring at me. He tried to smile but I immediately turned around. I didn't know who was supposed to feel more embarrassed between the two of us. It was his duty to be embarrassed, but it also was my right. I felt so stupid. How could I have thought that the prettiest boy in the school could really like me? And why, with the same ease, did I still believe that the most famous singer on Earth would one day marry me?

If there had been a subject called "Delusion" in my school report, I would have achieved the best possible mark. But if in the same report they had put "Logic", "Dignity" and "Intelligence", my average grade would have been heavily affected.

On my way home, I was thinking about the difference between reality and fantasy, wondering if it was possible to love two different men at the same time and in two different ways. I loved two men. One lived in the real world and I had tried to drag him into fantasy. The other one lived in a fantasy world and I hoped to drag him into reality. Maybe it was the Paduan covered walkways that made me rave, because they didn't allow thoughts to get out of people's mind. You felt constrained under those hanging tunnels.

I heard a bicycle bell. "Sorry!" I was almost hit by a bike coming from behind me. There were two bikes, actually.

"Miss Sferzaferri!"

"Alice!"

She looked surprised.

"Now that school is over, I really have to tell you: it is illegal to ride a bike under the porches!" and I burst out laughing at my new joke, just like my father would have. Then I noticed a man on a mountain bike next to her. Miss Sferzaferri saw me look and felt the need to explain.

"He is a friend of mine. We are going for a ride along the river." She was clearly eager to get away quickly and most of all to shift focus from him to me.

"Mauro, this is Alice Innocenti, my brightest student. I gave you a very good mark, didn't I? Are you happy?"

"Yes, Miss. Thank you!" Thinking about it now, I wonder why when students get a good mark, they are supposed to be grateful.

"Where are you going for your summer holidays?" she asked me, feigning curiosity.

"Same old plans." I started listing the things I would do, counting them on my fingers. "Tuscany at Nonna Tilda's, Sardinia with my parents, mountains in August. But the most important thing is this!" I added, bouncing excitedly. I rummaged in my bag, where I kept my passes 24 hours a day, waiting for occasions like this.

"I'm going to Croatia next week! My father got me two passes for the Take That concert!"

My teacher burst out laughing, a real heartfelt laugh.

"You made it, then. You're a stubborn girl! So, this means that if you marry Gary, we won't see you again at school in September!"

Miss Sferzaferri knew the names of all the members of the band. It was her way of showing that she cared about me. One day she had even confessed to me that she liked Gary too.

"Well, have fun, Alice!" The couple pedalled away, so I didn't have a chance to speak to Mauro. Then she shouted from the distance, "Alice! Maybe one day you should write a book about Take That! Think about it!"

Maybe yes, it was possible to fall in love with two people at the same time. Maybe Miss Sferzaferri loved Mauro and her husband, the same way I loved Tommaso and Gary.

The only difference was that Miss Sferzaferri was in the middle of a divorce.

# CHAPTER 20

## The Train

"Can you believe this?"

Roaring laughs and tears.

"What if he speaks to me, what am I going to tell him?"

"I don't know. You could just say, Hi Robbie, will you marry me?"

Roaring laughs and tears.

"When I see them, what will I do?"

"Pull up your shirt!"

Roaring laughs and tears.

"Which song would you like to listen to?"

"Put on *Back For Good*! No, wait … *Could It Be Magic*! No, no, no! Do you have *Why Can't I Wake Up With You*?"

Tape rewinding in the Walkman.

"How long does it take?"

Eyes looking outside the window.

"I don't know. It's taking too long! Would you like some chewing gum?"

Jaws chewing gum.

"This is our moment, Alice. Our fucking moment!"

"I know. It really is."

Eyes filling up with tears, hands intertwining.

"How's your mother?"

"She feels like shit, obviously. Just before I left, she looked me in the eyes and said, 'Go. This is your dream so it's my dream too'."

Eyes staring at each other. Sobs, hugs.

"She might not be there when I get back. It terrifies me."

Watery eyes.

"Bullshit. We'll be back in a couple of days!"

"Here it is. Come here."

Earpieces splitting. *Back For Good.*

"Ticket, please!"

Hands rummaging in the backpack.

"I've already seen yours, you excited little girls. How many times do you want to show them to me?"

Ticket inspector smiling.

"1 billion 22,000 watts." Had it been measured, that would have been our level of energy, happiness and excitement; all that electricity could have caused a short circuit on that Intercity train 9867 from Padua to Pula. It was June 21$^{st}$, 1994. A similar emotional phenomenon had been observed only in Woodstock back in 1969.

The man with glasses, who got on in Mestre, and the hairdresser from Udine, who were sitting next to us, were staring at us in disbelief. After witnessing such joy, they had probably realised, by contrast, how sad and boring their lives were. They could have attempted suicide. Or in the best scenario, they would have needed years of psychotherapy to rehabilitate their happiness.

By then, all the passengers in the train knew that in coach 7 there were two overexcited girls. Many of them peeped in, out of curiosity, to see what their teenage dreams looked like.

Laura and I had shouted, sung, danced, and sweated. We also had planned our final strategy. It was final because rather than thinking about how to dress for the concert, we were thinking of what to wear for our weddings at that stage. There were still 2 hours travel before the train arrived in Pula. Then we would go to the hotel and at 7 o'clock Raimondo Merletti's secretary would come and pick us up to escort us to the concert. Take That would arrive at about 9, for a "Meet and Greet" with the fans – us – before the concert. We would have the chance to touch them, hug them, talk to them and take some pictures with them. They would sign posters, caps, pants and bras. For the occasion I had brought a small pink bra. I wanted it to look credible.

We hadn't even bought the return tickets, because we believed we would fly back to England with them. I had said goodbye to my parents, bequeathed my school notebook to Matilda, called Nonna Tilda to say I loved her, and removed all the posters from the walls. I was sure I wouldn't need them anymore. They belonged to fantasy and would become useless compared to reality.

Laura had kissed her mother's bald head and bought a vase of tulips to be placed in the living room, to remind her mother of her love. She had taken her dog for a last walk and she had stopped by an estate agency to check the house prices in Manchester.

After all, we had our passes. Two tickets to a bright future. Two pieces of paper that originated from cancer. Raimondo Merletti's cancer. The cancer my father tried to heal. The cancer that was killing Tessa Islanda and that needed to be replaced with happiness, with all those things that those people could no longer do.

All we had to do now was wait. And the wait felt endless. The train stopped for about 10 minutes in Trieste.

"Isn't Tommaso from Trieste?" asked Laura.

"His father is, but yes, his relatives still live here. I guess he is here on holiday."

Laura stood up, lowered the window and waved her pass. "Fuck you, Tommaso Orpali!"

I laughed, even though I felt a bit like crying because, after all, I still liked him a little. We had left our situation hanging between the possible and the plausible.

I laughed, and as I laughed, I looked for him outside the window, as if I could have suddenly seen him run on the platform, ready to jump on my train. As if it were plausible to assume that he knew where I was, that he was thinking about me, that he was missing me. I kept looking for him and for a moment, I believed I had seen him. My heart stopped. But it wasn't him. It was just a boy with a rose in his hand, waiting for a girl who wasn't me.

The train started moving again. We fell asleep. When we opened our eyes, we were in Pula train station. Our journey was over and another one was about to begin.

# CHAPTER 21

## Take That

My imaginary camera operator, who specialised in shooting horror sequences, was waiting for me at the hotel. At 7 o'clock the imaginary cameras started rolling.

Laura and I took the lift, then we walked through the hall, through the journalists, the fans who had managed to sneak in and the flashes of the photographers. Bodyguards escorted us to a black-windowed car, like two real celebrities.

We were no longer two human beings carrying a backstage pass. It was more like the backstage pass was carrying the human beings. Laura was wearing her usual black dungarees, gel in her hair, ear piercings and a blue small nose piercing. I was dressed in white, like a bride. Long, waterproof, highly flammable trousers, white crop top. Nice degree of suntan. Loose and still wet hair. Clear lip-gloss and a touch of mascara. White G-string, visible through my trousers, which made more than one man stare at me.

The Pula Arena was magnificent, like the Verona one. It was packed with fans holding placards, surrounded by giant screens on each side. Light technicians were testing lights, illuminating the audience with multi-coloured and stroboscopic rays. Other technicians were tuning the instruments on the stage. Dance music in the background kept spirits sky high, while fans sang stadium chants dedicated to Gary, Mark, Robbie, Jason and Howard.

The imaginary camera operator kept on filming. Quick feet on the ground, passes bouncing on chests, hearts pounding, sweaty hands holding Laura's. Our silence within the noise around us. Security – that word had acquired a divine dimension for us – took us backstage through Gate 9. Then they escorted us along the narrow corridor beyond the Artists Entrance, up the stairs, through the amphitheatre's hidden mazes, and beyond the boundaries of reality, until we reached our Mecca. It was a room as big as a gym, with blue carpet and black walls, where they had set up a banquet and from where we would be able to see the concert through a huge glass wall.

"Stay here." Amanda asked us to wait and told us that we could eat and drink as much as we liked. However, our stomachs were tight, our hearts were in our throats and there was no room for food to pass through. No room for words. Time went by much faster backstage, almost at the speed of light, and we had to concentrate in order not to lose our balance.

"What about now?"

"Now is now, Laura."

How long can an instant last, if it is the instant that has lasted for a lifetime in your head?

Now we just had to try to relax.

A scene from the movie Airplane! crossed my mind. It was the scene where a woman has a panic attack during the landing procedure and a bunch of nuns slap her in the face, telling her to calm down; and the more they said so, the more the woman panicked. There is nothing worse than asking a shaken person to calm down. And we, just like the woman in the movie, were terrified.

"Alice!" Amanda called me.

We jumped from our chairs like cadets during their first drill.

"Calm down. They are not here yet."

I had always hated people who told me to calm down, together with cyclists and slow walkers.

I was listening to her carefully. Amanda went on, "I've watched your video. It's wonderful."

"What video? How? What?"

"You should have sent that to us earlier. It's authentic, funny, touching."

*"What video?"* The one I had thrown at Tommaso?

"A boy from Trieste came here this morning. He told me that he is a friend of yours and that you would have never had the courage to send the video. So, he took care of it." Then she added with a smile: "It's clear that you don't like the same music. He was wearing a Kurt Cobain t-shirt."

I was speechless. Laura put a hand over her wide-open mouth.

"I gave the tape to Take That's manager and they have just called me to ask your permission to use it for their next single. They are looking for footage that has been filmed by fans for their new song, *Never Forget*."

And, before I could either reply or give her my approval, Amanda walked off, headed to other guests with backstage passes.

We had to sit back on our black plastic chairs in front of the coffee table not to lose our balance. Before she disappeared again, Amanda approached us for the last time. "The summer internship offer is still on the table, in case you wanted to accept it."

Then she gave me a postcard.

"I almost forgot. The boy left this."

It was a postcard from Padua. I didn't understand. Laura snatched it from my hand and started reading it.

"What I want is not in Canada. I want you to know that what I really long for is here, and that here you will always find somebody who loves you. Tommi."

Canada? Padua? Love? He will wait?

I felt like I was about to faint!

Laura grasped a magazine from the table and used it as a fan. I couldn't process reality. Maybe I had spent too much time basking in fantasy. It was as if I had lost the basic tools I needed to face contingent events. A dysfunction of the auditory, visual and motor system. Maybe I had 'cancer of the pragmatic cells'.

I only had an intuition. Yes, it was possible to love two people at the same time. A real person and a fantasy one. And maybe it was possible to love just one person too, if he represented the joining link between the two worlds. I started singing Gary's cover of *How Deep Is Your Love* by the Bee Gees in my head. I also suddenly realised what was really going on. Take That wanted to use my video, so I started imagining *Never Forget* in my head.

At that point I could only express myself through songs. As I was singing the second chorus, the backstage area filled up with journalists, photographers and celebrities. The room was full of people looking for something to tell.

The amphitheatre roared. Somebody had just said something important into the microphone. Amanda stood up on a chair and announced: "Please, please, calm down! Take That are on their way! And if you can't calm down, at least pull yourself together!" Then she added: "Fuck!" before getting off the chair and fixing her skirt. We were like antibodies after a malaria attack. We all had to go back to our anatomical positions after a few moments of panic.

Dressed like a white Virgin Mary waiting to become a Magdalene, I was standing in front of the banquet table with my back towards the rest of the world. I could hear the camera operators and the sound technicians run frenetically back and forth backstage, I could hear the agitated production assistant shout at the dancers. I could hear the teenage girls, the mothers and the journalists coming and going, the sound of flashes, the heavy silence before a big emotion, the tuning of guitars, and the volume of the speakers that were being set on the stage.

It was as if that stage was waiting for me. For the occasion I drank a Sprite. My heart was beating like crazy drums. My hands were sweating around the plastic cup. *Breathe, Alice. Just close your eyes and breathe. If they come here, you don't have to turn around, because he is the one who will have to make a choice. And he will choose you. You've come so far, and you won't mingle with anyone else, rushing at him to get a meagre instant of attention. You would rather pass unnoticed and forget about him for good.* I was playing the most extreme teenage role. It was black or white, yes or no, now or never.

I was scraping the bottom of the cup with the straw. I had finished my drink, so I had no excuse left to stay away from the rest of the world. As the last drop of soda was running through the plastic tunnel to my mouth, everything around me stopped. Like silence before the storm.

They had walked in the room. Take That. They were there to take some pictures with the fans, as promised by Raimondo Merletti. I couldn't stop sucking that straw, as if I were still trying to find a drop in all that air. Maybe I had got lost, like that drop. Maybe the young Alice had been swallowed up and replaced by a new one.

Take That were backstage. Laura burst out crying. Gary was behind me. *Please, look at me. Start from my sexy bum then up my back to my hair, hanging down my shoulders like a waterfall. Set your eyes on my delicate hand and come to me. When I turn around, we will look each other in the eyes, and you will know that I am the one. Your woman. The love of your life.*

A hand tapped me on the shoulder.

I turned around in slow motion and after a 180-degree rotation, he was there in front of me. His eyes staring at mine. His green, sincere and deep eyes. He smiled relieved, as if he had just found something he loved and had lost.

"Alice?"

I nodded. What else could I do?

"Come with me."

# CHAPTER 22

## The Stage

He took my hand in his. It was warm, strong, and sensual.

"Quick!" he said.

I had spent so much time waiting, just to be told to hurry up. Years summarised in the blink of an eye.

He dragged me up the stairs leading to the stage, behind the black curtains, through electrical cables and the crowd of dancers, journalists, photographers, celebrities and fans, through indiscreet, curious and envious looks. All I could hear was fragments of voices, pieces of conversation, words.

"He chose her for the picture." "She's a fan." "Look at that girl!" "Take a picture of her." "You've got to interview her afterwards."

He turned around only once, before we got to the stage. "You are beautiful." He told me, as if he wanted to reassure me. Like a husband when you approach the altar. A promise of true love and protection.

Then he added in Italian, "Blissima," skipping a vowel. All of a sudden, he seemed more human to me, more normal, more possible.

He smiled again, in a sweet and almost romantic way. "I loved your video, you know?"

I couldn't speak a word, so I just winked. I thought it was the best answer I could give him. What was I supposed to say? "I love you, Gary. Please marry me?" I was like an actress who starts stuttering when they award her an Oscar. *Why are you stuttering, you moron? Weren't you ready for this? Don't tell me you're going to cry now.* Success-induced paralysis. No words came out of my mouth. Just silence. Like white, the sum of all colours.

Then the stage.

A wall of spotlights in front of me and beyond them a million dark silhouettes. The amphitheatre went quiet for a moment, but when we reached the centre of the stage, an incredible uproar of screams seized us like stretched arms. We held each other tight, so as not to be devoured. I could smell his cologne perfume mixed with the scent of his skin, which smelled like a biscuit dunked in baby food. He pulled me close, and it seemed that his muscles swelled up under his stage costume to protect me. He held my hands tight.

*I'm a bride. White-dressed in the centre of the church.*

I was completely confused. My head started spinning. I didn't know where to look, so my spontaneous reaction was closing my eyes and bowing my head.

*We are now out of the church and they are tossing rice.*

Lights were dazzling. Gary turned around and said to me "Look!" pointing away at the base of the stage. "Look there at the photographers."

*Mamma, Papá, come here. We need to take a picture for the album.*

"Ladies and gentlemen, this is Alice!"

The amphitheatre roared. I looked at the giant screen and saw that they were showing my video, accompanied by their last single, *Never Forget*.

Gary went on speaking into the microphone. Fans were delirious. "She made this!"

Yes, I had made that. They were all applauding me. I turned around to look at Laura who was standing next to Robbie backstage, weeping in a valley of tears.

"You are amazing! Thank you!" These were Gary's last words, as he gently turned my head with a finger under my chin towards the centre of the amphitheatre, where our picture stood out huge on the biggest giant screen.

*I now pronounce you 'husband and wife'.*

I stood still, between life and fantasy, between things that happen and things that may never happen, but could happen. As I looked at that picture, my whole life flashed before my eyes. In my not so awkward smile, I saw my innocent adolescence, the living room in San Frediano, Miss Sferzaferri and her divorce, my mother and her fitness, my father and the plastic of his Lancia, my friend Laura, who I met on the Teletext. I saw Tessa's cancer and the bishop's blessing, Gary's posters on the diamond patterned wallpaper, the car chases, the school tests, my Naj-Oleari hairband, the bad words I couldn't say, the cotton balls and the always immaculate pads, and Tommaso, with his fogged glasses inside the helmet.

It was a perfect moment: nothing could have ruined it.

But right in that moment, as 1 million souls and 20 million TV viewers were watching me, I unexpectedly felt that something was not going the right way. Actually, it was going only one way: it was going down, between my legs, and a tragic, growing awareness made me sense that, soon, the only person who would have kept on clapping was Nonna Tilda, from her living room in San Frediano.

All of a sudden, I felt a strange pain in my belly and frightful sensations. It was as if all my intentions and emotions, that had been stuck in a funnel for years, were now flowing like a cascade. Or worse; an unstoppable red river.

I was there, with my mouth open and a terrified look, like the main characters of horror movies who stay petrified and quiet before being stabbed in the shower. The characters who irritate spectators: *Do something, for Christ's sake! Run!*

Spectators surrounded me too and I couldn't run away. Gary was next to me. I hadn't been able to say a word yet. That was my last chance. I looked at him with imploring eyes.

The crowd and the worldwide broadcast were waiting for me to do something. Maybe now I could finally swear. He gave me the microphone.

And the only thing I could say was "Fuck, I'm wearing white pants."

# Acknowledgements

A special thank you to Helen Wraithmell, an exceptional, witty, competent English teacher and friend, who has helped me with the English translation, showing dedication, extreme patience and creativity.

I want to thank my friend Laura and all the Thatters of the world, who have inspired this book and shared my adventures, keeping a dream alive; my family, who wanted me to be a writer since I was a teenager, hoping that this would stop me from trying to be a tv presenter; my children, Giulia and Cesare, who cheer me up every day; my Facebook "readers", my best friends, who have spent a lifetime putting up with my poetic-philosophical-existential theories; my schoolteachers and my school mates at Liceo Ippolito Nievo for providing excellent memories which I used in the book.

Last but not least, I want to thank my first period, which showed up really late, preserving my innocence, for a while.

Never Forget!

# The Flow

In every organism, at whatever level, there is an underlying flow of movement toward constructive fulfilment of its inherent possibilities.

~ Carl Rogers ~

A HEART FOR AUTHORS À L'ÉCOUTE DES AUTEURS MIA KAPΔIA ΓΙΑ ΣΥ
FÖR FÖRFATTARE UN CORAZÓN POR LOS AUTORES YAZARLARIMIZA GÖNÜL VERELIM
PER AUTORI ET HJERTE FOR FORFATTERE EEN HART VOOR SCHRIJVERS TEMOS OS A
RT SERCE DLA AUTORÓW EIN HERZ FÜR AUTOREN A HEART FOR AUTHORS À L'ÉC
ВСЕЙ ДУШОЙ К АВТОРАМ ETT HJÄRTA FÖR FÖRFATTARE À LA ESCUCHA DE LOS AU
ΜΙΑ ΚΑΡΔΙΑ ΓΙΑ ΣΥΓΓΡΑΦΕΙΣ UN CUORE PER AUTORI ET HJERTE FOR FÖRFATTERE E
ÖINKÉRT SERCE DLA AUTORÓW EIN HERZ
ÇÃO ВСЕЙ ДУШОЙ К АВТОРАМ ETT HJÄRTA

# The author

Luisa is an international award-winning copywriter, author, blogger, mother and surfer. She has lived across four different countries including the UK, the US, Italy and Australia and worked at the most prestigious advertising campaigns as a creative thinker and writer.

She is a happy, adventurous, energetic Italian mother of two who loves exploring the world, creating meaningful relationships and investigating life in all its aspects. If she is not cooking lasagna, she is probably writing or surfing a wave!

# The publisher

*He who stops
getting better
stops being good.*

This is the motto of novum publishing, and our focus
is on finding new manuscripts, publishing them and
offering long-term support to the authors.
Our publishing house was founded in 1997, and since
then it has become THE expert for new authors and
has won numerous awards.

**Our editorial team will peruse each manuscript
within a few weeks free of charge and without
obligation.**

You will find more information about
novum publishing and our books on the internet:

w w w . n o v u m - p u b l i s h i n g . c o . u k

Printed in Great Britain
by Amazon